IF THE BROOM FITS

A WIT AND WHIMSY ROMANCE

SALLY JOHNSON

Copyright © 2021 by Sally Johnson
All rights reserved.
No part of this book may be reproduced in any form or by any electronic or mechanical means, including information storage and retrieval systems, without written permission from the author, except for the use of brief quotations in a book review.

This is a work of fiction. Characters, names, locations, events and dialogue in this book are products of the author's imagination or are represented fictitiously.

Edited by Danielle Williams
Cover design © 2020 LJP Creative
Published by Pink Bloom Publishing
Las Vegas, Nevada
First Edition 2021

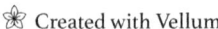 Created with Vellum

JULY

PROLOGUE
GRANT

I was now the proud owner of a...dump.

The ominous, avocado green Victorian-style house perched on a small hill, mocking my stupidity.

Did I buy this from the Addams Family?

I had an inkling of regret.

No matter how I looked at the house, whether from the east side or the west side, front or back, it was still a dump. And the attached garage looked strangely out of place. The ad called it a "charming fixer upper." There was no charm. Or the Realtor had a different definition of "charm" than I did. Either way, it was all mine.

Served me right for buying a house sight unseen and "as is". It didn't seem like such a risk at the time. After all, it was a great, affordable price. If only I had bought the house next door. It was also a Victorian-style house, but was obviously taken care of. It had a purple door, wrap-around porch, crisp gray paint and landscaping. It looked so much better, brighter, not so... abandoned.

Maybe it looks better inside. The interior rooms hadn't looked so bad in the pictures online.

I stumbled up the driveway towards the front door, careful not to trip on the oak tree roots ripping up the concrete from the bottom. The rest of the length of the driveway from the road to the slab of concrete was dirt, plagued by potholes and ruts and overrun by weeds and brush that made it difficult to navigate to the house.

That'll need to be replaced.

Maybe I should've invested in a plane ticket to Delaware and done a walk-through before finalizing the purchase. Even the smell of honeysuckle growing wildly up the side of the garage didn't ease my regret.

But too late. I was here and was going to make the best of it.

I pulled the neckline of my T-shirt and used it to fan myself. Was it always so humid in the summertime here?

The concrete front stairs were uneven. I grabbed a hold of the metal guardrail. It wiggled in my hand. Upon closer inspection, I could see it was practically rusted through at the base. The door was moss green and needed a fresh coat of paint in some other color, but I expected everything else in the house did too.

Taking a deep breath, I opened the front door.

Nothing happened. I grunted, elbowed my shoulder into it. Still, nothing happened. The door was stuck in the frame. I shoved it with a full body slam to get it to budge. It didn't move. That would need to be replaced.

The scent of I-don't-know-what, greeted me, like a smack in the face when the door finally busted free. It was a combination of old people smell, mildew, maybe death, and cat pee.

Cat pee! Crap! Midnight! How could I have forgotten Midnight?

In my stupor, I'd left the cat in her soft travel bag in the car. The vet had given her some pills to sedate her, since she hated confined spaces, crates, soft travel bags, car rides and pretty much everything else, including me. But I didn't have the heart to rehome her before I moved. Guilt played heavily in that decision.

She was probably still sedated, I reminded myself. She hadn't made a peep or a meow on the trip down here and because of that, I didn't want to disturb her. And it wasn't like she was going to die or suffocate if she woke up and was in the car alone for a few minutes. I had unzipped the bag enough to let her head poke out and ease my guilt of keeping her confined. But what if she was awake and frightened? I *should* get her out.

I hurried out of the house, careful to leave the front door open so I wouldn't have to wrestle it again. From what I could see through the car window, the bag looked undisturbed. I opened the backseat door quietly, careful not to wake her.

"Yeow!" she screeched, swatting a paw at me from inside the bag. She bolted past me, shot out the door, across the grassy driveway, into the open door of the house.

At least she ran into the house, I thought, tripping up the driveway after her. I closed the front door to keep Midnight inside, which required another full body shove. I rubbed my shoulder, regretting using it as a battering ram. The right side of my body was going to hate me tonight if I had to do that every time I came in and out.

I added "front door" to my mental list of things to repair.

"Midnight," I called out tentatively as I stepped into the small foyer. "Middy, Middy, Middy!" I sang. The room to my right was the dining room. There weren't many places to hide since it was empty. Of furniture, that is.

There was plenty of trash, and shadows perfect for a black cat to hide in.

I chose my steps carefully because there was dried poop on the floors. Poop on the floors?! Ugh! That hadn't been in the photos! *At least it's not fresh poop*, I told myself.

It was muggy inside and not from being closed up. The humidity freely entered through the broken front window.

Replace front window.

Broken front window!

I ran to it, peered out, but the light was going. If the cat had gone outside, I'd have zero luck finding her in the dark.

"Midnight," I called, slowly walking across the hall to the living room, stepping over chunks of drywall, empty bottles, trash.

What have I gotten myself into?

A card table was set up and a lawn chair beside it. Why was that there? Had it been left by the previous owners, brought in by kids trespassing, or owned by squatters? Did I have a squatter problem?

Check for squatters.

The carpet had seen better days. Even better years. In keeping with the theme of the house, it was a moss-green shag. In the front corner, some of it had been peeled back, exposing the padding, which was flattened and crumbly. I rubbed my foot on one spot and it disintegrated beneath my weight. Would it fall apart when I pulled it up? An image of a booger green, flaky mess came into my mind.

Rip up and replace living room carpet.

The back wall of the living room had fake wood paneling, in, you guessed it, moss green. Was that supposed to be an accent wall? That was going to have to go. At least it was just the one wall.

I swiped the sweat trickling down my brow with my forearm. I'd been out of my car for less than five minutes and the sweat was also trickling between my shoulder blades. I doubted this house had central air. I'd kill for an A/C unit right now. Would it help with the putrid smell? Would fresh air circulating change anything? Or was it something so bad that it would only be banished with a sledgehammer and a fresh sheet of drywall? Bleach, kitty litter, Lysol, Febreze. My odor-elimination options ticked through my head as my mind wandered to my cat. Midnight would be less than thrilled if she shared her new digs with feral cats and raccoons who might be reluctant to vacate their squatted living accommodations.

I climbed the stairwell, testing each step before I put my full weight on them.

The hallway led to the three small bedrooms, which were in no better condition than the living room. There were doors on the rooms, with holes in them. One door it was the top panel, as if someone had punched it, and the other door it was the bottom panel, as if it had been kicked in. The closet doors were nowhere to be found, and neither was the cat. After a cursory glance, I moved on.

"Middy, Middy, Middy!"

No cat.

The master bedroom was a little bit bigger than the other bedrooms, but not by much. A king-sized bed would consume the whole area. Good thing I only had a queen. Midnight could have hidden under this room's nasty stained double bed, if the beneath-the-bed crawlspace hadn't already been packed full of trash.

I turned my attention to the attached bath. "Midnight?" I asked. I looked around quickly, saw no signs of life, neither feline nor squatter, and quickly shut the door. The toilet had looked like it had been hit by a sledgehammer and the small sink had been removed from the wall and on the floor on its side, blocking entry. It was stained with rust. At least, I hoped it was rust.

Back in the main hall, the main bathroom was the next door down. The door was open a bit, and I pushed on it cautiously. This bathroom was intact, that is to say, the toilet and sink were still attached. The bathtub and surrounding tile were, of course, avocado green, and the grout was dark and stained. The shower curtain and rod were in the tub, along with dirt and debris.

The toilet lid was down and I didn't open it. I didn't want to know what was in there. Or what was on the walls.

The wall with the window was spotty and travelled up to the ceiling. There was a big, watered-down cola-colored stain the shape of Asia right above the sink. I had a roof leak. Great. And mold. Of what color and variety, I didn't know.

Please, please, don't let it be black mold.

The linoleum was peeling in some areas, and most notably, along the tub and the wall behind the toilet. Under the window and sink, it was lifted and dark.

I exhaled slowly as sweat trickled into my eyes. I squeezed them shut trying to get rid of the stinging. Maybe when I opened my eyes I would awaken from this nightmare.

I didn't.

I shut the door behind me.

Retracing my steps, I retreated downstairs to the front area of the house, thinking the cat may not have gone as far as I'd thought. Maybe she'd think her treats were in the kitchen.

Heart sinking, I continued making my way towards the kitchen, noting the awful blemishes of the house as I passed by them: holes in the drywall, disgusting carpet, graffiti, more broken windows, and water damage thanks to said broken windows. And that terrible, funky, disgusting smell.

The kitchen. An old fridge remained. For fear of what might be left in there and what it might smell like, I didn't open it.

The popcorn ceiling had only one water stain in the corner that backed the bathroom wall. Hopefully that meant a roof patch. But the popcorn finish would have to go.

The floors, like everything else, were disgusting. A gross goldenrod and avocado linoleum remained in places, but most of the edges had peeled up. I hope that would make the removal go easier.

Actually, the whole thing might be improved with some napalm.

I ducked down and shined my cell phone's flashlight into the cabinets, but they only had dirt and trash in them. I was out of places to look.

Midnight was gone.

And so was our nest egg.

I returned to the living room, sank down into the failing aluminum chair. Uneven, it kinked to the right and I almost fell over. After I recovered, I ran my hand through my sweaty hair.

Where to start?

I pulled out my phone and started typing.

Dumpster. Biggest one possible.

Roof. New one or just patches? Please be patches.

I paused, thumbs posed to type. I wasn't sure what to add next or even where to start.

~~Rip up and replace living room carpet.~~
~~Peel up and replace linoleum.~~
All new flooring.

The house listing didn't get into the important details. Like everything that needed to be fixed. How had I been so stupid?

I really wished I was friends with Chip Gaines right about now.

Find Home Depot.

Ka-ching. Ka-ching. Ka-ching rang through my head.

I heard a creaking and twisted quickly to look behind me, hoping it was Midnight and not a squatter returning, when the aluminum frame of the chair buckled. I landed on my back.

I picked myself up off the floor and located my phone, which had landed a few feet away.

Buy a new chair.

My plans needed to change. Originally, I thought I'd spend the night here and be ready when my furniture PODS were delivered tomorrow. I had a sleeping bag in my trunk, along with an air mattress, ready to "rough it" in the house. That was before I knew what a disaster this house was. With the stench, I couldn't stay here. I'd have to get a hotel room.

I went through the whole house again calling for Midnight, gave up and took my search outside. Maybe she'd escaped the house, but stayed nearby.

Please, please let her have stayed nearby! I'd never forgive myself if she got hurt out here.

While walking by the garage door, I noticed a half-open window above, just the right size for a cat to squeeze into. I gave the garage door handle a try; it was locked. There was no garage door opener or key with the keys I'd been given. Both keys went to the front door.

Hoping there was a chance the door wasn't really locked,

I gave it an upward tug, only to be met with resistance. The door wasn't moving.

Garage door guy.

I walked the perimeter of the house, shining my cell phone light around, getting more and more depressed. The back was worse than the front. Sagging rain gutters, broken basement windows, rotten wooden back steps, siding falling off or just plain missing.

Call a handyman was also added to the list.

And the yard was an overgrown mess of tall grass, weeds, bushes and trees.

Lawnmower, landscaping tools. Or find a landscaper.

In my search, I discovered why the garage looked so strange. It wasn't actually *attached*. *It had* been built about a foot away, which I was sure was against some building code these days, but who knew if it was when it was built. I hadn't noticed from the front because the overgrowth had hidden the gap. Midnight could be in that narrow space and there was no way I could even *try* to get her out. Without much hope, I shined my cell phone into the narrow space. It was just a tangle of weeds and dilapidated trellises.

I braved the smell of the house one last time in a Hail Mary attempt to find Midnight. I didn't know what to do. She could literally be anywhere.

"Midnight?" I called. "Middy, Middy! Here, kitty."

Just to be thorough, I checked all the nooks and crannies I could find and discovered a narrow door to the left of the fridge. It was the pantry I had passed over my first time around. A chunk of it had been taken out of the bottom. She could have squeezed in there.

I opened the door slowly, as I had learned everything in this house had to be done with caution.

There were no shelves, but stairs.

I had a basement?

I had a basement.

Should I celebrate or scream in fear?

The smell of damp earth filled my nose as questions flooded my mind. Was there even a remote chance that any part of it was finished? Was this where the body—or whatever was making that smell—was hidden? Did the squatters live down there? But most importantly, was Midnight down there?

With my phone's flashlight on, I tested the first step, gently adding some weight until I was somewhat sure I wouldn't break through. I repeated the process for all thirteen stairs.

The basement was *not* finished, but I realistically never thought it was. That would be too easy. The headroom was inadequate and I immediately whacked my forehead on a floor joist.

I cursed under my breath out of pain and frustration. It didn't hurt all that much, probably just a bruise, but couldn't just one thing be right in this house? Just one thing. Was that too much to ask?

The water heater was in one dark corner, the heating system in the opposite dark corner. The only light came from a small, two-paned window, that was mostly boarded up. I held my phone up, flashlight on, and panned the room. Under the stairs was a round flash of animal eyes, reflecting light.

"Midnight!" I said, exasperated and relieved. "You sure sent me on a wild goose chase." I carefully made my way to her across the dirt floor, keeping the light on the ground to avoid any unexpected surprises. I tucked my phone under my chin and reached with both hands to grab my cat.

"Grrr."

I stepped back. Midnight didn't love me, sure. But that didn't sound anything like Midnight.

The low, guttural noise came again. I took another step back and grabbed my phone before I dropped it.

I shined the light in the direction of the animal and two yellow, glowing eyes, surrounded by bristling, gray-and-white striped fur, stared at me.

Without a moment's hesitation, I ran up the stairs, taking them by twos, praying they wouldn't give way in my moment of need. I reached the top of the stairs, slammed the door and ran outside.

Once I was on the front porch, I stopped, gasping for breath, resting my hands on my knees. The air was so heavy with humidity, it felt unusually hard to catch my breath. Sweat ran down my forehead and into my eyes. The salt made them sting and I squeezed them shut briefly. I blinked a few times, used my sleeve to mop my forehead and leaned against the railing. I couldn't think.

The cat was not a cat.

It was a raccoon.

A snapping noise was the only warning I got. The railing gave way and me and the metal fell backwards into the bush. The branches snapped under my weight and I rolled onto the ground.

The search for Midnight had been a failure. Buying this house had been a failure. And there wasn't anything I could do about either problem tonight.

I went back to my car and shut the door after me.

1

KATE

The razor cut through the box top easily, making a "zip" sound as it went. I peeled back the flaps and was accosted by the scent of pumpkin spice.

"It's July fifth," I said out loud, even though there was no one around to hear. I was tired and grumpy from sleeping terribly the night before, thanks to the fireworks. "The fifth. This is ridiculous. We haven't even discounted the Fourth stuff." I looked into the box and pumpkin spice candles in the shape of jack-o-lanterns with weird toothy grins smiled back at me. I lifted one out. "I don't like you or any of your buddies in the box. If I had my way, I'd—" I stopped, sensing I was not alone.

I turned and confirmed I was, indeed, not alone.

He was about my age. Tall, wavy light brown hair that was shaggy but not long enough for a man bun. Deep blue eyes. And what looked like a goose egg above his left eyebrow.

"You're a girl," he said.

What gave it away? The double D's?

But if I got written up again, I'd be fired. So, I held my tongue, forced a smile and answer him politely. "I am."

"Sorry to interrupt your nefarious plans for those pumpkins, but could you help me?"

Helping him meant getting up off the floor and abandoning my assignment. These stupid jack-o-lanterns weren't going to unpack themselves, but I couldn't say that. Instead, I bit back the snark-laden comment and forced a smile. "Sure. I'd be more than happy to."

"Do you guys sell flashlights, uh, Katherine?" the man asked, leaning to the side to read my name tag.

Flashlights? Was he serious? Hello, you're in a building called "Hawley's Hobbies". What an idiot! Do you wanna ask for a belt sander while you're at it?

"Sorry, you want the Home Depot two blocks down," I managed in my customer service voice. Soothing and light.

"Oh. Right. Um...Well, maybe you can help me with something else. I need something called 'Mod Podge.'"

Shocked that he'd asked an actual legitimate question (for this store),

it took me a moment to unload the smart comment already loaded on my tongue. "Sure, Mod Podge, aisle five."

I held my smile in place five seconds longer than necessary and stood. I placed my ~~weapon~~ box cutter in my apron pocket so I wouldn't be tempted to use it on anything or anyone while on this errand. I rubbed my hands together, making a mental note to apply hand cream once I was done. Handling cardboard was very drying to the skin. But applying lotion while still working with the boxes could leave grease stains on the products. Which again, made for an unhappy boss. And an unhappy boss made for an unhappy Kate.

I took the lead and headed over the two aisles and

pointed him in the right direction. "Down there on the left." I turned to return to my pumpkin purgatory,

"Wait."

I froze.

"I have a question. I'm hoping you can answer."

As was I.

I slowly turned on my heel to face him again, fake smile back on my face.

He was holding two containers of Mod Podge, one in each hand, as if literally weighing the difference.

My phone buzzed. Loud enough for him to hear it because he looked like he was trying to locate it. I pulled out my phone, silenced it, slipped it back into my pocket and looked around to see if Robyn, my boss, was anywhere in sight. She always seemed to show up the moment my screen lit up. She wasn't. *Thank you, Crafting Gods.*

"This is it, right?" he asked.

My phone buzzed again. I didn't break eye contact with him for two seconds before giving in. The screen lit up my pocket with an eerie glow. I nodded for him to continue.

"There's so many different—"

My phone chimed, signaling a text message. Then again. And again.

He pointed in the general direction of my phone. "Do you need to get that?"

I held up my index finger, then pulled my phone out. "Sorry, I forgot to shut it off." I held up my index finger, then pulled my phone out. I swiped the screen and glanced at it.

3:01 P.M. Missed call. Becky.

Becky had worked with my sister, Chrissy, at Gainesville Amusement Park a couple of years before. Chrissy introduced us, and we'd been friends ever since. Why was she calling? She knew I was at work.

3:02 P.M. Missed call. Becky.

I switched over to my messenger.

3:02 P.M. **Becky:** 911!

3:03 P.M. **Becky:** Kate?

3:03 P.M. **Becky:** Call me ASAP!

I powered it down quickly and looked back at the man. "You were saying?" I added a winning smile for good measure.

"There's so many different ones." He turned back to face the shelves. "Have you ever used this stuff?"

I stiffened. "Yeah, I've used it." Three years ago. Hadn't touched the stuff since.

"Should I get matte finish or glossy finish? What's your opinion? Matte? Glossy? Yes? No?" He lifted each bottle in the air with every other word.

His question drew me further into the aisle since I couldn't carry on the conversation from the endcap. My right hand gripped my phone in my pocket, itching to call Becky back. Instead, I sighed, knowing this might not be a quick conversation. "Depends on what you're doing."

He laughed and it sounded borderline nervous. "Actually, I don't really know *what* I'm doing, if you can't already tell."

Well, now that he mentioned it. But who was I to point out the obvious?

As he examined the bottles, he continued. "I'm trying to de-coop-age, or something like that, a map onto a piece of wood."

For a moment, a wave of compassion washed over me, but it left as quickly. Poor guy stuck in a craft store. "What, did your wife send you on this errand?"

"Like four years ago. I'm just getting to it now."

Procrastinate much? "At least you're getting to it. Is she not crafty? Or is this a project you promised to make and never did?"

He stilled briefly. "You could say that."

"Now that you're getting to it, I'd suggest matte unless you want it shiny. With paper and stuff, especially a map where you might want to look at it closely, you don't want glare."

He set the bottle of glossy back on the shelf. "Matte it is."

"You don't take much convincing." Thank goodness. Most customers thought about it longer, some even debated with me, which I found very annoying.

I wanted to get away so I could call Becky.

"You obviously know what you're doing, so I'm treating you like the expert," he said.

He wasn't wrong. At least technically speaking I could still be considered an expert.

Without warning, he leaned in a little closer. "You look familiar. Have we met before?"

As a knee-jerk reaction, I leaned back. He was in my space. "Nope. Doubtful. I'm antisocial."

He laughed at my comment, but I really *was* serious. I didn't socialize.

"You look like someone my wife used to watch online. YouTube, I think. Some crafty lady. Karen or Casey or something."

"Kate?" I offered, wondering if I was correct with my guess.

He snapped his fingers. "Yes, that's it. But you're..."

Fatter than I used to be. "Taller than her?"

"Maybe that's it. Her hair was black too, I believe."

It *was* black, but I hadn't kept up the color. Now it was back to its natural mousy blonde.

"You know who I'm talking about, right?" His eyes met mine, searching for affirmation.

I nodded. "I know exactly who you're talking about."

He wasn't wrong.

And neither was I.

He was talking about me.

"If you're done, I'll walk you up to the counter and grab some foam brushes along the way." I took a couple of steps before pausing to make sure he was following me, coaxing him away from the shelves and the conversation.

"Do I need foam brushes?"

"Definitely."

"Why?"

Why? Asks the man who can't even pronounce decoupage.

"Because it goes on smoother and leaves less brush marks."

He made a noise, satisfied by my answer.

Once he was beside me, I led the way, giving him pointers about decoupage and foam brush advantages as we walked. I made sure we passed Robyn, the boss, and that I said hello for good measure. Never hurt to have your boss see you treating a customer right.

At the front of the store, I spotted some flashlights on an endcap by checkout.

"Oh, look, we do have flashlights. And a great selection." I reached up and pulled a five-inch, bedazzled flashlight that was essentially useless off the rack. "It's pink, cute and puts you in touch with your feminine side."

His lips pursed. "Think I'll try Home Depot instead."

I hung it back up. "Good call. They might even have headlamps."

I don't know why I said that. It was just that goose egg on his head. How did that happen?

His fingers went to the bruise and he touched it lightly. "Maybe."

"Anything else I can help you with?"

His eyebrows were up and his voice was hopeful. "Humane animal traps?"

What exactly was this guy up to? Flashlight, animal trap and decoupage? Was he into some weird flamboyant taxidermy? Squirrels with sequined ten-gallon hats?

He sensed my confusion. "You know, for trapping strays and raccoons and things."

It was those "things" I was worried about.

"You might need to buy that online. I don't think, we, or even Home Depot can help you with that."

He shrugged. "Doesn't hurt to ask."

I just nodded and walked him to a checkout lane.

He turned to me as I was leaving. "Thank you so much. I don't know what I would've done without you."

A crappy job that would end up balled up in a trash can. I'd been witness to such carnage many times. "Just remember you don't want to apply a top coat until the map has dried a full twenty-four hours. Otherwise, you might rip the thin paper."

There was another nervous laugh. "Good to know, because I'd do that and probably ruin the project."

I waited as he paid, surreptitiously powering up my phone while it was still tucked away. I needed to get back to the horrid pumpkin spice candles, but counted watching him check out as working. You know, like customer follow-through by making sure he was completely taken care of before I returned to aisle three. A quick glance at my phone told me I didn't have to return but could instead take my afternoon break. I swiped the screen and punched in my PIN.

My co-worker, Celine, walked up behind me. "How come you get all the attractive customers?"

My arm dropped to my side and I put a step between us, because again, personal space. "What do you mean?"

She nodded her chin toward the automatic sliding doors. "That guy you walked up to the check out."

I caught a glimpse of him as he exited the building. In my opinion, he wasn't particularly memorable. My type was tall, dark and Italian. He was *not* my type.

"Oh, him. Pretty sure he was married." I turned toward the back of the store, anxious to take my full break. And check my phone. And have a snack.

She followed and I quickly figured out she must have the same break. "So, he was attractive enough that you checked his ring finger." Her voice became teasing.

I shook my head, realizing I hadn't done a ring check. "No. He was talking about his wife."

"Still not fair. You're not even interested in guys." She kept pace with me all the way into the break room.

I held up my index finger. "Correction. I'm interested in guys. I'm not interested in dating. There's a difference." I grabbed my bottle of water from the fridge and sat down at one of the two circular tables in the dingy room.

"Doesn't seem like there is. I've worked with you for two-and-a-half years and I've never heard you talk about dating." Celine took the seat opposite me.

My chin lifted up a notch and I shrugged. "It's not the right time." I hoped she too would want to check her phone on her break, or have a snack, instead of talking the whole time.

"When is that? When all the planets align perfectly? Or when Mercury is in retrograde?"

I laughed, but it came out sounding more like a snort. "Mercury is always in retrograde in my life."

"Oh, hey, my daughter's birthday is next Saturday at two\ if you want to come. You could bring a date."

"Sorry, I'm busy." It was an automatic response.

"I also wanted to ask if you had any suggestions to decorate for her party. She's turning two and we're doing a Disney Princess theme."

Why was she so chatty today? "Have you checked Pinterest? That's the best go-to, in my opinion." Not that my opinion should matter, but she seemed to think it did.

"Funny thing, I went to Pinterest and found a video you posted on YouTube."

That's why she was asking. "Did it help?"

She lifted a shoulder. "It was a little dated."

Yes, it would be.

"I'm looking for a fresher take. Do you have any good ideas?" She leaned forward and waited.

"Keep searching Pinterest?"

"You don't have *any* suggestions? What would you do if it was your party?"

I shrugged. "Not throw one."

I checked the clock hanging on the faded, pistachio green wall. "Well, break's over. Delightful talking to you. Back to the stupid jack-o-lanterns and pumpkin spice."

"You seem pretty passionate about that."

I pushed my chair back from the table and it made a satisfying scraping noise against the brown linoleum meant to pass as laminate wood flooring. "It's July fifth. Society has taken this pushing-the-next-holiday thing way to soon. What about poor Labor Day? It's being completely overlooked because we're setting up for Halloween in July."

She squinted at me. "How does one exactly decorate for Labor Day?"

"I don't know, barbeque—" I shrugged but didn't think about it too hard. My eyes slid over to the door, mentally planning my escape route. I squeezed my fingers around the silicone phone case.

"You totally know, and don't deny it!"

I forced myself to look back at her. Her smile declared victory.

"I used to know, but I don't care anymore." I tried to sound bored. "I have better things to pour my energy into, like fighting Halloween in July." With that, I grabbed my empty water bottle, compressed it with both hands so it became a quarter of what it was. It made a loud protest.

"Let me know how that fight goes," she said.

"Will do." I pulled out my phone. If I was quick, I might be able to call Becky before returning to stocking shelves.

"Kate? A minute?" It was Robyn. She stood in the doorway, her boss "uniform" of too-tight khakis and an unflattering, boxy t-shirt undermined my ability to trust her decisions.

My phone went back into my pocket and I arranged my face in a neutral expression. Then added a smile for good measure. "Of course."

Talking to my boss vs. unloading pumpkin spice candles. Which was worse? It was a toss-up. Definitely Robyn. Although I mentally reviewed if I'd had any "missteps" since the last time she needed "a minute". That had been about a customer complaint that I'd seemed "reluctant to help her." Nothing came to mind.

"Walk with me."

Ugh. I hated that expression.

"A wedding planner emailed us earlier. Kelly something."

I made the appropriate "paying attention" noises.

"She's in charge of a celebrity wedding this fall."

Celebrity? Fancy. But why would they be doing it *here*? We were a small, nowhere town in Delaware.

"I'd like you to be her personal shopper."

I stopped walking and turned to her, confused. "Why?"

She stopped also, since it'd be hard to continue the discussion if only one person was moving.

"Because I want her to know we are professional and can treat a famous person the way they are used to being treated."

I didn't care about how a famous person *thought* they should be treated. "No. I mean, why me?" I was by far, the worst employee.

Robyn's chin dropped and her eyebrows inched up slowly. It was her *knowing* look. "Because you're the most capable."

You got that right.

"I don't know, Robyn."

"Listen, Kate. There's a lot riding on this."

This was her family's store. She was third generation. It was one of the rare brick and mortar stores that hadn't yet succumbed to chain store take overs or online shopping. And, like most family-owned businesses in smaller towns, it was surviving, but that was it. Not thriving, not dying. I got her concern.

She continued. "And you and I know you are more than capable of—"

"That's not my thing anymore." She knew it, I knew it, former fans knew it.

Her voice dropped. "This is important. This could put us on the map."

On the map? Most people had never even heard of our town. The only landmark was Gainesville Amusement Park which was nowhere near as famous as Disneyland, nor would it ever be.

"But—"

"Uht." She made a guttural noise to stop me. "No excuses. I need you to do this. And to sweeten the deal, if you do a good job, I'll give you your choice of shifts *and* a raise."

Money. More money was always a way to get someone to do something they didn't want to do. Including me. But more money didn't entice me to jump at a chance to help a wedding planner. Now my choice of shifts, that was another story. Would I prefer opening or closing? Or, even better, could I get off the rotating shift and have a fixed one? Now *that* was appealing.

I exhaled quietly. I really, *really* didn't want to. But a set schedule? I gripped my phone in my pocket, itching to call Becky. "Fine. I'll do it."

2

KATE

I grumbled all the way to the car.

I should've been happy to get a special assignment from Robyn.

I'd get the shift I wanted.

Maybe even less time spent prematurely stocking the shelves with Halloween things.

A raise.

But being the personal shopper to a celebrity wedding planner? Nope. No way. Weddings made me ill. Bad juju. I turned the TV channel if a wedding came on. I could pull over and puke right now. And sometimes helping the celebrity herself? What would *she* be like? Bridezilla? I strived to keep my life devoid of high-maintenance people, stressful situations and emotionally draining experiences. It was simpler that way.

Once I climbed in and slammed the door, I blasted the A/C. Then I fired up my phone and hit Becky's number, only to have it go straight to voicemail. Figures. Why didn't she text me what was so important? Now I'd to keep wondering *and* think about my new work assignment.

Personal shopper. Hmmt!

Having to pretend to be interested in someone else's wedding would be exhausting. One-on-one-time encouraging wedding ... whatever, left a bad taste in my mouth.

Maybe the couple would wake up to the fact that our town was dull and not a destination wedding spot and change locations. My mood lifted ever so slightly.

As I carefully navigated the back roads, looking forward to getting home, I decided to hope for the worst. Weddings got canceled all the time. The thought placated my stress level just a bit.

I lived about ten minutes outside of town. Other than the house immediately next to me, the land on either side of the houses was undeveloped land populated only by trees. Where my backyard property line ended, a field lay beyond and finally became a wooded area again. All in all, it was about ten acres of natural insulation.

I liked it that way.

Pulling into my driveway, I smiled as my plum-colored Victorian house came into view. The recently installed solar carriage lights created a warm glow on either side of double-wide garage door.

Home sweet home.

My front door opened and then closed without as much as a knock or a doorbell ring to give me notice. I jumped forward from where I had sunken into my couch and reached for the remote. But I was five seconds too late. And I almost kicked my piping hot Hawaiian pizza off the coffee table in my haste.

My younger sister, Chrissy, announced her arrival with a

question. "Why are you watching Christmas videos on YouTube?" She brushed her dyed-black hair off her forehead and I could see her raised eyebrows.

I quickly flipped the channel to whatever was the next channel higher.

"Jeez, Chrissy! Haven't you ever heard of knocking?" I quickly flipped the channel to whatever was the next channel higher.If she had come five minutes earlier, she would've caught me staring out my window at the Haunted House next door. I swear I'd heard something, like a slamming door or window. She probably would've accused me of eavesdropping on ol' Haunty.

Her hand went to her hip. "But then I can't catch you checking out a certain someone's YouTube channel."

"I'm not." I pointed to the TV screen, where a very buff man in black stretchy shorts was doing crunches. "See?"

She pushed her glasses up and made a show of checking out what was on the TV. "You're watching Extreme Abs on Steroids?"

I wasn't sure if that was the name of the show, but the guy definitely had extreme abs and looked like he was on steroids. And the moves he was doing was something I'd never manage. Or even attempt. "I was thinking I should start exercising."

"Ha, you so *were* watching the Mistress of Christmas!" Her cry was triumphant. And also, annoying.

Sometimes she was too smart for her own good. And I was too proud to admit I really *was* watching that. Or, more accurately, Merry Webber. I opened my mouth, but Chrissy continued.

"Would you stop torturing yourself? It's been three years. Three. Years." She settled in beside me, but only for a moment. She leaned forward, getting a closer look at my dinner.

"I'm not torturing myself." The denial was strong with this one.

"You are," she argued. "Can I have a slice?" She reached for one without waiting for my answer. Trying to hoard it all to myself was futile. I nodded in defeat.

"You are." She blew on her slice. The aroma of melted cheese drifted past my nose.

"Okay, I had it on. Big whoop. Sometimes I feel like checking out Christmas in July."

"Oh, please, Kate. I'll give you a minute to come up with a better excuse." Chrissy took a tentative bite. When the food proved edible, she completed the action by ripping the tip of the slice off with ferocity.

I inhaled deeply, then exhaled loudly. I was too hungry to offer a feeble excuse. "Hand me that slice of pizza, would you please?"

"Get it yourself." She motioned to the rest of the pie with her slice. "You just said you needed more exercise. Now's as good a time as any."

"I changed my mind."

"But today could be the first day of a new you."

I stuck my tongue out at my little sister, but her back was toward me so she didn't see, so I said, "If I cared, would I be thirty pounds overweight?"

I stuck my tongue out at my little sister, but her back was toward me so she didn't see.

"Probably not," Chrissy replied, then made a noise of approval. "This is good."

And that was some of the blame for my weight gain.

A light flashed in my windows.

"What was that?" Chrissy asked, standing up.

My heart immediately beat faster. Were those boys back? "A flashlight?" I joined her at the window, looking out into the dark. The only thing out there was an abandoned house.

"Do you think it's a person?"

"It's certainly not a ghost," I replied. The only thing out there was the abandoned house. It wasn't haunted. At least not that I knew of. "Sometimes teenagers like to sneak in there and graffiti it. Or drink."

Chrissy looked expectantly at me. "Could it be squatters?" Chrissy looked expectantly at me.

"I sure hope not. I haven't seen any activity. If there were squatters living there, I'd assume I'd see someone coming and going."

Chrissy raised her eyebrows. "Maybe they do it while you're at work."

I rolled my eyes at her. "I doubt it."

She pulled the curtain back again. "Are you going to call the cops? It could be someone breaking in."

I laughed. "To Haunty? I doubt there's even a lock on the door. And what would they steal? He's been abandoned for years."

"Maybe they wanted to break into your house and got confused." She put her hand on her hip, her tone sassy. "If the person is on drugs, they're not exactly in their right mind."

It had been almost two years since I had called the cops on some teenagers who had egged my house. My heartbeat quickened a little just thinking about it. "True."

Chrissy continued narrating what she saw. "The light's now in the house. I think it's looking for something."

I debated for a second if I should call the emergency or non-emergency number for the police. I held the phone in my hand, my finger hovering over the screen.

"The flashlight just went into the backyard," Chrissy narrated.

I hit "3". It could just be—

"Wait! It's walking toward your yard!"

Without waiting, I backspaced and then dialed 911. My heart thudded against my chest. Why was someone looking around my backyard? Was it a drug addict high on something and confused? Kids messing around? A homeless—

"911. Do you need fire or police?"

"Police."

"Hold."

I took a few quick breaths.

"Police. What's your emergency?"

"This is Kate Coughlin," I said, exhaling quickly. "There's someone in my backyard with a flashlight."

"Is this person armed?"

"I don't know," I said, suddenly anxious. I hadn't considered that. I couldn't see anything but the light the flashlight gave off. They very well could be armed. "They were originally in the neighboring house."

"What is the address?"

I quickly spouted off my address, then Haunty's for good measure.

"A car has been dispatched and is en route."

"Thank you," I said. I joined Chrissy, who was now at the kitchen window over my sink. "They're on their way," I whispered.

"Good," she whispered back.

"I'll stay on the line until the officers arrive," the dispatcher said.

"Alright," I said. "Thank you."

We remained in tense silence, watching the glow of the

light make erratic patterns in the grass. The beam suddenly shot up and shined right into the window.

"Agh!" We yelled in unison, stepping back away from view.

The light went out immediately.

Chrissy sunk down to the floor with her back against the cupboard. I followed suit, then decided to crawl across the floor to the tiny space between my fridge and the cabinets and pulled out my broom.

"Do you think they're going to come up to the house?" Chrissy whispered.

"I don't know. I hope not," I whispered back. Would I have to be a human shield to protect my sister?

"If he does, are you going to beat him with the broom?" There was a hint of doubt in her question.

"Hey, a broom is better than nothing."

The wail of a police siren could be heard off in the distance and I exhaled the breath I'd been holding. "They're here," I whispered into the phone and hung up without waiting for further instructions.

I made my way to the living room window. Not one, but two cars came, the lights flashing in my front windows and reflecting on the ceiling. Must've been a slow night in the town.

Three flashlights made their way to the side of the neighboring house. I watched, waiting. A knock at my front door startled me, and I peeked out the peephole, relieved to see an officer.

I pulled open the door. "Hey, Bruce," I said, happy to recognize a guy I went to high school with. "Come in."

"The other officers are checking next door. I'll be back to let you know what we find."

"Thank you," I said. Knowing Chrissy and I could safely

watch from inside helped my breathing calm down. Hopefully they'd get the person and it'd be over.

After a few minutes, the group of men gathered by the porch.

"That was quick," Chrissy commented, straining to see what was happening out in the dark. "Would it be bad to open a window? I'm dying to hear what's going on out there."

I shook my head. "Let's wait here until they come tell me it's okay."

"I don't hear much of a struggle going on." In fact, I heard no struggle. I took that as a positive.

"Kate?" Bruce called through the screen door, jarring us from our rubbernecking.

I walked back to my front door. "Hey, yeah. What's up?"

"We didn't find anything or anyone. Maybe it's those kids from before, but if it was, they left awfully fast."

That seemed so . . . benign. "Huh."

Without meaning to, I laughed. It must have been a result of coming down from the adrenaline. "I'm sorry." I waved an arm, trying to justify my odd behavior. I forced myself to put my hand down. It ended up across my heart. "I feel so ridiculous for calling. Or maybe I'm just so relieved that you checked it out for me."

"Alright, then. Take care, Kate."

"Will do," I said, my voice higher than normal. Again, an after-effect from the adrenaline, being overly perky.

We both flopped on the couch. I was suddenly exhausted and assumed Chrissy probably was too. "Thanks for coming over uninvited tonight," I said, allowing my head to loll on the back of the couch.

"I'll make sure I do it again sometime soon."

"Okay. Want to stay the night?"

"Sure. Do you have any ice cream?" Chrissy's head tilted toward me.

Did I have ice cream? Like she needed to ask. "Yeah. Black raspberry or toffee crunch?"

With a groan, she sat up straight. "I'm just going to help myself to the carton. Do you want a spoon?"

"Please," I said.

Chrissy returned less than a minute later with both half gallons and two spoons. "Here's to a crazy night," she said and handed me the black raspberry ice cream and a spoon.

We clinked spoons as if toasting.

"What would you've done if that guy tried to get in here?" Chrissy asked, licking ice cream off her spoon.

"I don't know. Have you run out the back door in the kitchen while I beat him with the broom?"

"What if that didn't work?"

"Try blinding him with Lysol?" I was coming up with this plan on the fly. Even saying it out loud, it didn't sound very plausible. I was really glad I didn't have to actually enact the plan.

"Can Lysol be used in self-defense?"

I shrugged. "I dunno. Never tried it. But if it was the closest thing handy."

My sister patted my knee. "Even if it didn't work, I'd appreciate your valiant effort."

"You're my sister. Of course, I'd protect you."

A scratching at the back door paused the conversation.

My breath hitched in my throat. *Was he back?*

Chrissy and I looked at each other.

"...Haunty?" Chrissy said, eyes wide.

Yeah, it may have been silly, but it was better than thinking that the cops hadn't just missed some weirdo outside our house.

"Are you going to check that out?" Chrissy asked.

"Heck NOOO!"

"But you're the older sister! And it's your house!"

"Haunty's not my house."

The scratch came again. *Skree, skree, skree!*

"C'mon, Kate, you know it's not actually Haunty borrowing a cup of sugar."

"Maybe it's just a branch in the wind." I really hoped that was true. Really.

The eerie scratching came again.

We both turned and looked toward the back door.

Dread gripped my chest. What if the Flashlight Felon was back, but without the flashlight? Did I dare open the door?

I put the empty ice cream carton quietly on the table, then I tip-toed through the kitchen. For the second time that evening, I grabbed my broom.

"Don't you think a kitchen knife might be more appropriate?" Chrissy whispered into my ear. She had somehow snuck up behind me, and in doing, scared the bejeebers out of me.

"Chrissy!" I hissed, spinning around to face her. "Don't do that! I almost wet my pants."

"Sorry. I just thought it'd be better if we were together. You know, you with the broom, me with the Lysol and the knife."

I turned around. "You grabbed a knife?"

She held it up. It glinted in the light. "Sure did."

"What about the Lysol?"

This time she shook her head. "I don't know where you keep it."

"It's under the sink," I said, pointing.

"Should I grab it?"

The quick succession of scratches answered Chrissy's question and she dove for the cupboard. She came up with the Lysol, poised to spray. I held my finger up to my lips to signal Chrissy to be quiet, then proceeded to the door, gripping the broomstick. My hands were so sweaty I was worried I'd lose my grip if I had to beat off a perpetrator. My heart pounded as I took a quick peek out the glass pane.

I didn't see anything, which was way better than I expected.

I exhaled and took a few deep breaths trying to steady myself. I flipped on the porch light and looked out the door window. I couldn't see much and the dim, fifteen-watt light bulb did nothing to illuminate the area enough to investigate.

With a deep breath, I pulled the door open, frantically sweeping the broom side to side. The bristles made contact with something and I saw a weird black shape dart into the bushes before it let out an unearthly yowl.

Chrissy screamed and I jumped back.

I slammed the door and pressed my body against it for reinforcement.

"What was that?" Chrissy's breaths came out in puffs.

"I don't know, but it's gone." I took a second to make sure I hadn't wet my pants.

"I can't deal with any more excitement." Chrissy stood and grabbed her purse.

"Don't leave me!"

Chrissy was already at the door. "You got your Lysol and your broom!"

"Stay! Please. You can sleep on the couch." There was an ounce of truth to my begging. I had two spare bedrooms, but I hadn't let anyone into them in three years, not even family.

"If I can't sleep in a bedroom, I'm not doing it," she said playfully. She knew that was her out.

"But my couch is super comfy. C'mon!"

She waved my request away and stepped outside. "You don't need me. You'll be fine."

"But I do!" I said, just as the door slammed behind her. Seconds later I heard her engine roar to life and my sister peel out of the driveway.

"Fine, ya yellow-bellied excuse for a sibling!" See if I ever acted like her human shield again!

I locked every door and window in my place—even in the rooms I hadn't dealt with—then locked myself in my room with a chair shoved under the door handle. The broom came with me to bed and the Lysol was on my nightstand ready to blind any intruders.

It was going to be a long night.

3

GRANT

When I returned to "The Mistake", I was careful to do so in the daylight and to park on the tiny concrete patch. In plain sight of my neighbor.

My first mistake last night was thinking I could find my black cat in the dark. My second mistake was parking on the tree-lined road where nobody could see me. Like a psycho. And my final mistake was shining my freshly-bought flashlight into the neighbor's windows. Like a stalker.

No wonder they'd called the cops on me.

Granted, I was just looking for *my* cat on *my* property. Crossing the property line was unintentional, given all that crazy overgrowth. I gave up the search after I inadvertently peeped in my neighbor's house and hustled back to my car. When I heard the police sirens, I flat out ran. Immature, I know, but I panicked.

I scared my neighbor, though, and I should apologize. In the daylight. I didn't want to start things off on the wrong foot with my closest—and only—neighbor.

I got out of my car, squared my shoulders, and marched over to the neighbor's place to make things right.

Tap, tap, tap. I leaned against her railing, waiting. It did not get past me that her railing didn't fall over at the slightest hint of weight.

"I've got a broom!" a female voice said from the other side.

Okay? And how was I supposed to respond to that? "Hi, um, my name is Grant and I'm your new neighbor."

Silence.

"I was here last night and I think I scared you," I said to the lavender door. "So I wanted to apologize."

Whoosh! The door whipped open.

My jaw dropped. "Katherine?" From-the-craft-store-Katherine. She was in a faded, flannel bathrobe, and her long, wet hair hung in her face, but there was no mistaking those blue eyes.

She did, indeed, have a broom in her hand. What did she plan to do with it? Beat me? Brush me away? Chase me off the porch with it? I took a step back.

"That was you?" she said. There was no acknowledgement that we had met before.

"W-w-well, yeah, but it's all a misunderstanding," I stuttered. This was proving more difficult than I imagined.

She folded her arms across her chest, the broom still clutched in her fist. "That's what all the creeps say."

"But, see, that's the thing. I'm not a creep."

Her eyebrows went up and her mouth set into a straight line.

I waited a few beats for her to say something more, but she contributed nothing to the conversation. "Anyway," I stumbled on. "I didn't mean to shine the flashlight in your house. I was looking for..."

My words were drowned out as a huge red pickup with a lift kit barreled down my driveway, practically skimming over the overgrowth and the potholes. I watch in awe and envy. I needed to get me a truck like that.

"Looks like someone with low self-esteem just pulled up," she said.

I looked between her and the truck. Did I continued with my feeble explanation or go talk to the handyman?

Katherine's glower remained.

Handyman for the win. Anyone had to be nicer than her.

But I'd return, armed with a better explanation.

"I'll stop by—"

BANG.

She'd shut the door in my face. I exhaled, glad to have an out from that conversation. I hurried back to my yard.

The man who stepped down from the truck looked about my age, early thirties, but with a beer belly and a farmer's tan. "Hey there, Mr.—" the guy glanced at a sheet of paper. "Shepard. I'm Bill Donaldson, the handyman you called yesterday."

"Hey."

We shook hands.

He nodded to the door. "You said you had a garage door that was stuck? Should we see what we got?"

We walked over and stood in front of the door. "I can't get it open from the outside," I said. "I turn the handle and it does nothing. A garage door opener didn't come with the property, so I think it's safe to assume there isn't a garage door opener installed."

"Is there inside access? Or a door around back to get into it?" Bill looked around to see for himself. He patted the corner of the garage. "This looks like it was an addition."

Which would make sense why it looked like it didn't belong with the house. It'd been an afterthought.

I would've felt foolish if I'd called someone and then they discovered a back door, so I had already checked all potential access points, both from inside the house and from the back of the house. "Nope. I checked everything."

"So, you're ready to take desperate measures?" said Bill, with an eager glint in his eye.

I winced. How much was this going to cost me? "Like breaking down the door?" I had considered taking a sledgehammer to it, but I didn't have one handy. I had also, but just for a moment, considered backing into it. Garage doors are notoriously flimsy, the aluminum crumpling at the slightest brush from a car. I learned that as a teenage driver. Why not bump it?

The easy answer was then I'd have to replace it and I didn't want to add that to my growing list of expenses. If I could get the garage opened with minimal damage to the door, it would probably save me a couple hundred bucks.

"No. I'll grab a couple of things from the truck. I can probably release the emergency pull handle without too much difficulty."

Release the emergency pull handle. Now that was something I hadn't thought of.

Within a minute he was back with a wire and fishing it through a seam. I mentally kicked myself for not YouTubing it first instead of calling a handyman. But, in my defense, I didn't have internet access out here.

A simple tug and he said, "That should do it." He nodded to the handle. "Want to do the honors?" He nodded to the handle.

I mentally kicked myself for not YouTubing it first instead of calling a handyman. But, in my defense, I didn't have internet access out here. "I hope it's not off the tracks," I said.

But the door lifted without too much trouble. Hopefully, there'd be no more complications. I needed the space to store my stuff, especially now that I'd seen the condition of the house. And the storage PODS were scheduled to arrive later this afternoon.

The sunlight revealed what the darkness hid and I stepped back in horror.

"Oh, man," Bill said, scratching his beard.

The garage was completely packed.

Full.

4

KATE

I got a new neighbor?! And it's Mod Podge man?!

How fitting that a creepy, stalker guy with a weird bump on his head moved into Haunty.

I know my co-workers said he was cute, but with that bump on his head and his behavior last night, he was also kind of a creepy stalker. Curiosity got the best of me.

I decided to ~~spy~~ observe while I ate my cream cheese-laden bagel on the couch beside the window. As I pushed aside the curtain, the sun glared in my eyes. I squinted, trying to get a better look.

Along with the red monster truck, there was a dark green Subaru Outback in Haunty's driveway.

What was going on over there? Did Mod Podge Man seriously rent that house? In that condition? Was he stupid? Was it even habitable?

I'd considered, for like a moment, buying the place myself, but I didn't reno anymore. It was easy to realize how ridiculous that idea was and to completely vanquish it from my mind.

The only reason I considered it in the first place was

because it was located so close to my house. There were no other houses for at least a half a mile on either side of me. Owning the house would guarantee my solitude.

Maybe Haunty would scare him away and he'd be out of my hair soon.

A blast of "Oh, I'd love to be an Oscar Meyer Weiner!" interrupted my thoughts. It was my ringtone for Becky, left over from her days of working as a dancing hot dog.

I startled, almost dropping my bagel on the chair. Instead, it landed on the leg of my bathrobe, cream-cheese-side down. *I hate it when that happens.*

Shoot. In all the chaos last night, I'd forgotten to call her back.

I swiped my phone. "Hey," I said. "What's up?"

"Why didn't you call? Didn't you get my text?" She sounded breathless.

How to explain? I called the police on a flashlight felon? I went with a different excuse.

"When you texted, my boss was assigning me a special project and my new neighbor was wandering around in my backyard in the dark with a flashlight. I ended up calling the cops. Sorry, I meant to call you."

"You heard, then?"

I rolled my eyes. I obviously *hadn't* heard. "Heard what?" I obviously *hadn't* heard.

"The news?"

I waited.

"About a certain ex-boyfriend."

Sean. My stomach tensed and my breathed hitched. I took me a second to even want to ask the question. "What's the news?"

"He's getting married. Didn't you see it on Facebook?"

I exhaled. "I haven't been on Facebook for months."

That was part of my old life. "Who's he marrying?" I asked, even though I was pretty sure I already knew the answer.

"Who do you think? Merry Webber."

The Mistress of Christmas.

I hated her.

"Maybe he'll actually show up this time," Becky said.

"Only if he's grown a pair since last time."

Becky laughed. "If he hasn't, then she deserves it."

I chuckled along with her, because I assumed he hadn't changed. "Thanks for the heads up."

"Yeah, figured...well, I didn't want you blindsided. Again. Sorry."

I ended the call and checked the time. I had an hour before I left for work. It was one of the benefits of my job, business hours started at nine a.m. Instead of hopping up and hurrying to shower and get ready, I looked out the window again. As much as I wanted to check out what was going on, I would eventually have to go to work. I dreaded having to work on that wedding assignment.

I set my phone, face down, on a fiddle pie crust table beside my chair. I had rescued it from a dumpster behind the grocery store. The finish had been ruined by condensation rings made by drinking glasses, so I had painted it a nice gray chalk-finish paint. I found that was the easiest way to cover up a number or variety of flaws in a piece.

If only life could be chalk-painted.

5

GRANT

There was barely enough clearance for the garage door to lift without catching something. The same putrid scent that permeated the house hit us full force, and I took a few steps back.

Whap, whap, whap, whap, whap!

A cloud of black flying creatures swarmed out.

I swung my arms around my head to keep whatever it was from attacking me. I turned and ran and finally slowed down as I neared Bill's truck. Standing close by was Bill, bent over with his hands on his thighs, catching his breath.

He straightened, the took off his baseball cap and wiped his receding hairline with his forearm. "Dude, you've got bats," he said breathlessly.

Dang it! I was hoping it was birds. Couldn't I at least get some sort of break from this house?

"What do we do now?" I asked. I had no experience with bats. Do they go find someplace else to live now that I disturbed their lair? Will they actually attack me if I go into the garage? Will they come back?"

"Get tested for rabies? Bats carry rabies," Bill said. "And

you should get an exterminator out here to check the rest of the house and sure your attic is okay."

Raccoons! Bats! Rabies! Crap! There was no way I was sleeping in here until I got it checked out.

Call an exterminator.

Call the CDC.

We waited a few minutes to see if any more bats came out before taking a closer look.

I was probably the new proud owner of a whole family of raccoons. But no other animals or mammals appeared. All that was in there was remnants from someone else's life.

"Looks like the last people packed but forgot to take their stuff," said Bill.

I stared at the contents. There were boxes, newspapers, rusty bikes, furniture, and piles of clothes. That was just what I could see in the front.

How could someone move and not take their stuff? Where was I going to put my stuff if my garage was full of someone else's stuff? I'd have to store my belongings until I got rid of theirs.

I ran my hand through my hair as I tried to make sense of the situation. "I guess."

"What are your plans for this place, man?" Bill asked.

Good question. I wondered that very thing as we spoke. Fix it up. That was the idea before I saw it. But now as it loomed in front of me, it was a total gut and not just some patches. "I needed a project."

He whistled. "You definitely got that."

"And way more than I bargained for," I murmured. "I'm screwed."

"You ever fixed up a house before?"

I shook my head. "Nope. First time." *I'm so screwed.*

"Investor? Or investor and laborer?"

"All of the above."

"Are you in the building business or . . . ?"

"Nope.

"You going to live in it or flip it?"

"Live." If I could manage. I had no experience in home ownership, home repair, fixing up, flipping. Nothing. The most experience I had was the HGTV shows my wife used to watch. Those shows made it look so easy. And fun. Sure, there was usually some major problem that cropped up and threw the original planned budget out of whack, but I went into this planning on something like that happening. But ten thousand might not be enough contingency. I didn't plan on my fixer upper being a total dump. Or to be fulfilling this dream alone.

Bill looked directly at me. "You're telling me you bought this house for a first-time fixer upper project with no experience? Man, you *are* screwed."

"I should've stuck with the houses that only needed updating. Cosmetic stuff like new cabinets, countertops and removing wallpaper."

Bill pointed to the roofline of garage. "Roof is sagging." Then he squatted down by the foundation, his finger running over a line that snaked down like the Mississippi River. "Yeah. This one might be bordering on structural repairs. What did the home inspection list?"

"Didn't do a home inspection." More mental kicking going on with the admission.

He let out another whistle, this one long and slow. "No home inspection? Dude, that was a mistake. You *always* do a home inspection."

Hindsight was confirming that.

Bill walked to the backside of the garage and I followed.

We took really high steps since the grass was up to our knees.

"Did you check how long it's been on the market?" he asked.

That might've been a good idea and I regretted not doing that. "Nope." The price alone told me there'd be some work to do. Didn't realize just how much.

Bill scratched under his baseball cap. "I'm thinking, if I remember right, it's been at least a year. Maybe two by now. Can't recall exactly. It's always been one of those houses that seems empty and perpetually on the market."

"Do you know why the former owners sold it?" He was local, he might know.

"I think the original owners were elderly and passed away." He stopped and looked up at the roof above the small bathroom window. He pointed. "Roof's leaking."

Which was my assumption for the inside of the bathroom and the peeling linoleum.

"The house remained empty and the family finally decided to sell it," he said. "Or maybe they rented it out for a while and then decided to sell it."

At least a mass murder hadn't taken place there and it remained empty and eventually abandoned because of the ghost of murdered people. My imagination was getting carried away.

"So, you're a novice at all of this."

"Yeah. Lived in the city, never owned a house. Wanted to get out of the rat race and have a slower-paced life."

"And this is your answer?" The doubt in Bill's voice reflected the doubt I felt.

"It was supposed to be."

He pulled a business card out of his wallet and passed it to me. "Listen, I might be assuming too much, but it sounds like you need help. I have someplace I gotta be soon, but give me a holler later. I can help. I do a lot of this kind of stuff and what I don't do, I know people who do."

I held his business card in my hand, running my index finger along the edge. No doubt about it, I was going to need help.

I watched with envy as Bill barreled toward the road. Not for his truck, but that he got to leave this mess.

I turned back and stared into the abyss of clutter called the garage. If I could just get it cleaned out, it'd be a load off my mind. But as I looked at it, trying to figure out the best way to tackle it, I really just wanted to take a nap. But I had no bed and there wasn't any time for that.

There was so much work to do and I hadn't even started working on the actual house.

But right now it felt like the biggest job loomed in front of me.

The PODS were being delivered in the afternoon.

I'd scheduled the dumpsters, but delivery was at least a week out. It'd be smarter to empty the garage directly into the dumpsters, but I needed this space. It would be twice the work, but I had no other options.

So, for now, I'd empty the garage, leave the junk on the lawn, unload the PODS into the garage and then clean up the yard when the dumpster arrived.

Maybe Bill would want to help clean out my garage. But did I want to spend my renovation money on manual labor? I'd better just do it myself.

Without further thought, I pulled on my work gloves.

Some dream this was turning out to be.

6

KATE

Crash! Clunk! Crunch!

What was that awful racket going on over there? Even with my hair wrapped in a turban that partially covered my ears, I could hear it.

All the crashing and banging brought me to the window. I hope he wasn't going to be a loud neighbor. That wouldn't be cool.

I watched as bikes were literally thrown out of the garage and into a pile. More and more stuff flew out. It was like a dog digging a hole under a fence and the dirt was flying out behind it. I made a mental note to buy a high-quality pair of binoculars. This was fascinating.

I grabbed my work polo from the laundry room and pulled it over my head and came back to watch more garage clean out. I checked the time. I wasn't going to be late. *Yet.*

Who knew one garage could house so much stuff?

I pinned on my name tag and braided my still-wet hair.

Bang!

I took a closer look, curious to see what else was being hurled from beyond. What I saw stopped my heart.

Oh!

Even from my house, I could tell it was a Waterfall dresser. I loved anything Waterfall—the rounded edges, the beautiful the tones of the wood, the Bakelite handles. This was my favorite style from the Art Deco period.

Mod Podge Man shoved it onto its side on the lawn. What was he going to do with that? Throw it out? I had an internal war going on: should I take a closer look or ignore it?

He emerged from the garage with a sledgehammer in one hand and dragging a trash barrel in the other.

No! No! No!

I jammed on my flip flops and yanked the door open. "Noooo! For the love of all things vintage, don't do it!" I yelled, waving my arms wildly. I had to save that piece. It would be an atrocity to throw something so beautiful out.

He blinked at me, his face wrinkled in confusion. "What?"

"That! Piece, okay," I panted, positioning myself in front of the dresser. Whew! That was a workout. I gasped for more breath. "Don't break it up. It's a Waterfall."

He wiped a dirty hand across his forehead, leaving a dark smear. "So?"

"So?" My jaw went slack. He didn't just say that, did he? "So, it's beautiful." Did I have to state the obvious?

He squinted at me, his head cocked to one side. "Let me get this straight," he spoke slowly. "I come over to apologize about last night and you'll barely talk to me."

Suddenly I felt a little foolish for my earlier behavior. "That's the past."

He continued. "But I pull out a nasty old dresser and suddenly everything's okay?"

I pointed to his hand. "It could be if you put down the sledgehammer so I know you're not going to bludgeon me.

He shook his head and let go of the handle.

I ran my hand across the top. "But this is a 1930s Art Deco Waterfall furniture with all the original Bakelite hardware." The cedar veneer was loose on the edge, one of the handles was hanging by a screw (an easy fix) and when I opened the top drawer, and I could see one of the dovetail joints had been repaired with glue. But still, it looked pretty good for its age.

As I walked around the dresser, I caught a glimpse of inside the garage. I couldn't see much, because the windows were boarded up and the only light source was the open garage door. But from what I could see, the junk pile outside was going to get a lot bigger.

"I don't want it." He pointed to the water marks. "It's stained and probably smells like the garage."

"So, you're just going to discard it?" *Upgrade for a newer, prettier "piece"?*

"I have my own furniture."

Oh. The beauty of this piece had me coveting. Oh, but it was a pretty sin.

"Do you want it?"

Was he for real? Yeah, I wanted it. I wanted it so bad I was salivating.

I nodded like a bobblehead.

"You can have it," he said.

I didn't *need* it, though. I shouldn't do it. I hadn't worked on furniture in a couple of years. "Like have it have it or like sell-it-to-me have it?" I wasn't going to pay money for a project I probably wouldn't get to. But I could at least *rescue* the furniture. At least, that's what I told myself.

"Either you take it or it's going in the dumpster once it gets here."

I inhaled sharply. His words literally hurt my heart.

"Some pieces can be highly collectible." Usually ones in better condition, but I still had to be sure he was making an informed decision. I didn't want to take advantage of his ignorance.

"I don't care," he said.

"You can't throw this in the dumpster."

"Then you better take it. Do you need help carrying it over?"

A little burst of giddiness erupted inside. "No, I have a hand truck I can load it onto. I'll be back in a minute." I tore across the grass through the trees, leaping over the short hedge that ran along the property line. I had to be fast because I should've been leaving for work right. Now.

I held my breath as I searched for the hidden key to my She Shed in the flower box beside the door, paused, when my fingertip made contact with metal. The key was still there! Although there was no reason why it *wouldn't* be, I still had a moment of doubt. I fished it out, inserted it into the lock, turned the handle and pushed in.

A plume of dust rose as I swung the door open. I coughed and stepped back outside, letting the dust settle before re-entering. The hand truck was easy enough to locate in the back corner, but the tires were flat.

This was taking too much time.

But what if he changed his mind?

I could still make it to work on time. Or almost on time.

It took longer to find the tire pump, which ended up being in my garage. Soon enough the tires were pumped up and I was running across the uneven soft ground, the hand truck bouncing off-kilter to the neighboring yard. I had a moving blanket rolled up and secured by a bungee cord tucked under my left arm. I wanted to protect the piece from any further damage.

By the time I got there, I was breathless. It had been a long time since I had that much exercise. But it was also from the thrill of possibility.

7

KATE

I sped the whole way to work.

I justified breaking the speed-limit because I saved that dresser. It was so worth it.

My sense of elation was quickly slashed by the expression on Robyn's face when she met me at the door.

"You're late," she said.

The sliding front doors shut right as she said that and it created a sense of impending doom.

Yes, I was. I could explain, but she wouldn't understand. "I'm sorry. I got delayed."

She motioned with her hand to walk with her. "Kelly the wedding planner is here."

I scanned my memory for conversations regarding this. I didn't remember being told there was a meeting. "Was it scheduled?" And I just didn't get the memo? Or ignored it?

"Not exactly. I got the call this morning." She pursed her lips momentarily. "It's unprofessional to keep people waiting."

"Let's not keep Kelly waiting any longer." I hoped my "cheerful, can-do" attitude would soothe my boss's irritation.

"Meet us in my office," Robyn said.

Robyn veered off toward her office and I walked quickly to the employee lunchroom and threw my stuff in my locker, then hurried to Robyn's office.

There was a thin, tidy man topped with a side-parted bouffant of platinum blond hair sitting in the chair beside Robyn's chair.

Turns out, Kelly was a man.

Robyn could've given me the heads up.

Both he and Robyn stood when I entered.

"Kelly," she said, "this is Katherine. She's going to assist you today."

He squinted at me for a moment too long, as if trying to place me, the he stood, and reached out his hand. "Nice to meet you, Miss Katherine."

He was taller than I imagined when I first saw him. He was wearing a pink blazer with a white t-shirt underneath, and a pair of chambray-colored slacks.

"Same." I heartily shook his hand, pretending to be enthused. I grabbed a clipboard, some lined paper and a pen. I had to at least create the illusion I was interested. "Shall we?" I asked, even though I had absolutely no clue what I was supposed to do with him.

"Let's," he said.

If I'd had an assignment like this three years ago, I would've totally geeked out. I probably would've created a vision board, or a vision book, and carefully cut out sample items from our catalogs to create a presentation.

But I had nothing even close to that. Not a single clipping, not a single list, just a few sample items set aside in a shopping basket. I was going to have to wing it.

"First stop, my idea basket." It was left in a back corner

of Robyn's office, collecting dust. "I've put together a few basic items that we can check out."

Thankfully, Robyn didn't join us, but stayed in her office.

We walked toward the front right corner of the store. "We have a beautiful selection of white flowers that would add to any wedding." White equaled wedding. I figured I should be safe.

He flicked his wrist. "Oh, honey, I see where you're going with that, and it's actually in the wrong direction. I'm sorry, I should've informed you sooner. The bride is going a little non-traditional and wants a fall color theme."

I walked away from the display wall of white flowers in black buckets and over to the oranges and reds. I smiled, but was really gritting my teeth. "Meaning she'd be looking for more of a fall foliage flower theme?"

He spread his arms out wide and made the shape of an arch. "We need flamboyant."

"Flamboyant?" That wasn't usually a word used to describe a bride. I needed to nail down exactly what kind of person I'd be picking for. "Do you mean colorful? Over-the-top?" Over-the-top I could do. Or at least, used to be able to do. Now, I'd have to dig deep to deal with it. At least, temporarily.

"Dramatic. All of the above." He stepped closer and dropped his chin. "She's what I'd call a competitive personality. She wants her wedding to be bigger and better than anyone else's."

"Between you and me, she sounds like Cool Whip," I muttered.

"Cool Whip? What do mean? Sweet and fluffy?"

"You know, she has to top everything."

He broke out in laughter. "Never heard anyone described like that before."

He found it so hilarious that I started laughing. I wish all my co-workers and a certain boss had a personality like his. He was fun.

It took a second for me to regain my composure before I continued. "Okay, so we're looking for over-the-top."

Kelly became invigorated. "You know it, girl! She described it as fall with a splash of Halloween."

My heart literally stuttered, then started pumping overtime. I leaned closer to him, because surely I'd heard him wrong. "You said fall with a splash of Halloween?"

"Yes."

My wedding theme had been Halloween with a splash of fall. What were the chances? Maybe she was a fan? Or a superfan? Or a stalker?

That was so weird, but maybe I was reading too much into it.

I took a few cleansing breaths. *In through the nose, out through the mouth, in through the nose, out through the mouth.* "So, we're talking pumpkins, and taper candles..." and ghosts from the past. Or at least that's how it felt. *A splash of Halloween.* So weird.

A prickly feeling in my fingers made me realize I was gripping the basket handle. I looked down at the white silk roses, the white satin table runner and the rolls of glitter tulle ribbon and knew this was not your ordinary bride.

"Miss Katerine, are you alright? You're looking a little...pale."

"I'm, um, thinking..." or overthinking. Something was off. Granted, I was not the only one to ever have plan a Halloween wedding, but there was a little niggling in my gut, that was sending freak out signals to my brain, that was causing heart palpitations.

A splash of Halloween.

I squared my shoulders and cleared my throat. "Pumpkins are this way," I said. I set the basket on a random endcap, knowing I'd probably be the one who'd have to retrieve it and put back everything in it.

We went through and chose different items and Kelly snapped pictures to send to his client.

Once he walked out the exit, I checked my watch. That meeting had taken an hour and fifteen minutes of my shift and I was exhausted. And frustrated. And completely freaked out.

I raced around the store until I tracked down Robyn. "This isn't going to work out," I said.

"Walk with me," Robyn said.

Ugh. I was tired of walking. And for the last half-hour, I'd been mentally weighing the assigned task vs. benefits of having a set schedule. Was it really worth it?

Nope.

"I'm going to step down from the special assignment."

Robyn shook her head. "Not an option."

"C'mon, Robyn. I hate wedding stuff. I hate doing other's wedding stuff. Surely there's got to be someone better than me that can do this." That might actually be *excited* to do it.

Robyn halted, inhaled, and then exhaled. "Whether you admit it or not, you're not living up to your potential. I need you to do this. So, dig in deep and pull that old Kate out and make magic happen."

She must've *had* me confused with Tinkerbell. I couldn't just wave my little wand and "make magic happen."

This wasn't the Wonderful World of Disney.

This was Delaware.

I hightailed it to the bathroom, since I wasn't on break for another thirty minutes. This couldn't wait. I walked so fast people probably thought I was about to have a bout of diarrhea.

I sat down on the toilet, fully clothed (I know, disgusting) and sent a group text to Becky and Chrissy.

Me: 911!
Becky: ??
Chrissy: What's wrong?
Me: Emergency meeting at my house! Tonight! 6:30.
Becky: But you live out in the Boonies!
Chrissy: Are you going to have pizza at this meeting?
Me: Yes.
Becky: More info?
Chrissy: Pineapple and ham, please.

~

I arranged with Chrissy to pick up the pizza on her way over. That way Becky couldn't complain too much about the "drive." She pulled in right behind Chrissy.

"What's this big emergency?" Becky asked, swinging her purse as she walked up the stairs of my porch.

"Honestly, you had me at pizza," Chrissy said, carrying in two pizza boxes. She acted like she was only interested in the food, but Chrissy had a knack for seeing things clearly and I frequently sought her opinion.

I took the boxes from her hands and could feel the heat on the bottom. They smelled good.

"The weirdest thing happened at work today," I said as we all sat around the table. Chrissy flipped open the pizza box and helped herself to a slice. The cheese stretched as she took a bite.

Becky's eyes widened. "Okay," she said. "What was it?"

"The wedding planner I've been assigned to work with said his client's theme was Fall with a splash of Halloween."

Chrissy stopped chewing. "Wait. Wasn't that your theme for your wedding?"

I shook my head. "Close, but no. Mine was Halloween with a splash of fall. But isn't that weird?"

"Kind of too close to be a coincidence," Becky said.

"That's what I was thinking," I said.

"Who is the bride? Do you know?" Chrissy asked before proceeding to start eating again.

"I don't know. It's supposed to be a celebrity, right? But who?" I asked.

"We need to find that out," Becky said.

"Exactly," said Chrissy.

Hmmm. Would Kelly dish on his client?

8

GRANT

It had only been two days, but I was back knocking on Kate's lavender door.

She answered wearing a black and white polka-dot apron. It was on, but the ties hung by her side. Huh, I didn't picture her as a domestic diva. On the other hand, the interior of her house looked *and* smelled noticeably better than mine. Spaghetti sauce. Italian food.

But I wasn't here for dinner, I needed a plumber. And fast. "Hi, again. It's me. Do you know who to call to get the water shut off? I can't reach Bill—my handyman." My breath came out in pants.

"Try 1-800-SHUT-OFF-WATER," she said.

I had my phone out on the double. "S...H...U...T..."

"Ugh!" She scoffed. "That was a joke!"

I should've known it. It was too many letters. *Idiot!*

"Come on, please! My house is flooding! I need help." My shirt was soaking wet, as was my hair. Water ran down my forehead and into my eyes. I swiped at it with the back of my forearm.

She took a deep breath and rolled her eyes. "We don't have to call anyone."

"We don't?"

Another eye roll.

She took her apron off and slipped on a pair of flip flops. "Come on, show me where the leak's at."

Thank goodness for a capable female neighbor.

As we crossed the yard, she always stayed about two steps behind me.

I slowed my pace. "The water got turned on Friday night," I said. "I had the crazy belief that the faucets would work perfectly when I turned them on. They didn't."

We kept walking; I kept talking. "Today I noticed a small puddle on the floor in front of the sink. When I opened the cupboard under the sink, there was an even bigger puddle. It had obviously been dripping since it'd been turned on."

There might've been a small exhale noise on her part.

"To complicate things, I took matters into my own hands trying to fix the leak. It sprayed when I messed with it, then broke when I tried to retighten it." This DIY thing really means Damage It Yourself, I decided.

A snort? Possibly a *hmmt*. Then...silence.

She did nothing to keep the conversation going and I was out of conversation starters and antique furniture. When we crossed the property line, where my grass was out of control, she watched the ground where she stepped. *Was she looking for something? Snakes?* When my foot sunk in a muddy hole, I understood.

Grant

She pointed to the water running down the stairs. "You definitely have a leak."

I opened the porch door and slammed my shoulder into the front door. Why'd I close it anyway? It would've made more sense to leave it open and let the water run out.

"You really should fix that door," she said as she stood behind me. "Wait 'til it rains. It'll swell and you'll never be able to get it open."

"Thanks for the tip." It was already on my list of things to do.

When the door broke free, with a scraping protest, a steady stream of water ran out.

"You could've told me to wear boots," she muttered.

"I could've, but what fun would that have been?"

"This is not fun." She carefully took long, deliberate, tiptoed strides towards the kitchen, a squishing sound coming from the saturated carpet with every step. She squatted down by the cabinet, reached under the sink and miraculously, the water stopped.

"How'd you do that?" I asked, awed and surprised at the same time. Water still flowed past my feet, but the stream had slowed enough that the anxiety over the river in my kitchen settled. Should I take it as a bad sign that the water ran toward the front door? Downward. Another problem to consider for another time.

She pointed under the sink. "There's a shut-off valve is right here."

I bent down beside her so I could see what she was pointing to. "Where? Just so I'll know next time."

She leaned out as I leaned in. "Hopefully there won't be a next time."

I pulled my phone out of my back pocket, turned on the flashlight and shined it under the sink. I finally saw the T-shaped handle she was talking about. "Okay, I see now." It was red and hard to miss, except for an inexperienced eye such as mine.

I was close enough to her to smell her laundry detergent. It was a fresh scent I imagined would be called Hawaiian Beach at Sunset or something crazy like that. I leaned in, inhaling deeply. She was literally the best smelling thing in this whole house. Including me. I sniffed my arm pit.

"Are you sniffing yourself?" she asked.

I looked at her, realizing she had looked back right at the exact moment I took a whiff. "I'm worried I smell bad."

Her brow creased for a split second before she stood up and smoothed her denim shorts with her hands. "You got bigger problems than just B.O. You're going to need a plumber to install a new trap, you definitely need new gaskets and basically the whole assembly. But for now, that should do it. Good luck."

Good luck? She was just going to...

I turned to her and inadvertently shined the phone flashlight in her face was I moved.

"Dude," she said and her hand sprang up to shield her face. "That's bright. Cut it out."

"Sorry." I angled the phone downward. "I'm just surprised."

"About what."

"That you'd just leave. What about the mess?" The carpet was waterlogged and the linoleum floor was still a lake.

She was almost at the front door already.

"Could I possibly borrow a mop? Or some towels?"

She harrumphed and spun around. "You are the neediest neighbor I know."

I offered a cheeky smile. "I'm you're only neighbor."

She blinked. If she was impressed by my wittiness, she wasn't showing it. "How about a wet/dry shop vac?"

She didn't strike me as a girl who would have a shop vac, but what did I know? "Even better. Can I grab it now?"

"It's in my garage."

We once again crossed the property line and went to her garage. She punched the code in on the panel by the door and waited as the door lifted. I watched in awe as the inside of her garage came into view. It was clean and organized and *empty.*

She went in and rolled the orange and black cannister vacuum onto her driveway in less than a minute.

"Here," she said.

I stood there, stunned, completely overcome by garage envy.

She pushed it toward me with her foot. "Here," she said again.

I put my hand on the shop vac "You're a life saver. Are you sure you can't come over for a minute?"

She looked at me like I was crazy. "And what do you expect me to do? Sit down on the furniture you don't have and play get-to-know-you games?"

I mentally evaluated my living room through her perspective. True, there was only one chair to sit in. I had purchased a plastic Adirondack chair on one of my Home Depot runs. I decided to pick up a second one. Not necessarily for her to sit in, but for when I had guests. Like…Bill.

It had been quiet for a beat too long. I grasped for something to say.

"Can I at least thank you? Maybe take you out for a drink?"

She scoffed. "No thanks. I don't date."

"It wasn't intended to be a date. It could just be two neighbors getting to—"

She rolled her eyes and inhaled like a bull before it charged. "Know each other? No thanks." She had made her way to her front door by then. "You gave me the dresser. Call it even."

I couldn't leave it there. She turned to go back inside. But before she closed her door, I called after her. "Thanks, Katherine!"

She whipped around to me. "Kate!" she shouted, scowl on her face. "My friends call me Kate."

"So now we're friends?" I asked.

"Yeah, sure, whatever," she said. Then she slammed her door behind her.

I startled. Then grinned. *You don't know it, Kate, but I just figured something out about you!*

9

GRANT

Kate Renovates.
That's who she was.

I knew I knew her!

I was almost certain it was her.

When she said her name was Kate, it clicked. I was pretty sure my wife used to watch her on YouTube. And now I needed to confirm it.

I settled into my plastic Adirondack chair, pulled out my laptop and used a stepladder as my drink holder.

A few strikes of the keys and clicks of the mouse and I had found exactly what I was looking for: Kate's old YouTube channel, *Kate Renovates.*

I never paid much attention back when my wife watched the show. But that and HGTV had one hundred percent put this idea in my wife's head that renovating an old house would be fun. Renovating and "fun" were not two words I would equate together any more. Just cleaning out that garage made me want to place a "For Sale" sign on my front lawn. And I hadn't even tackled the inside yet.

I pulled up the first video, and witnessed a very different Kate. Yes, her hair was dark, dyed purpley-black which complimented her light skin and her blue eyes and she was thinner, but that wasn't the standout difference.

It was just...*her*.

She giggled, she joked, she had a self-deprecating sense of humor when it came to her mistakes. She seemed happy.

Video one she tackled the landscaping. She stood in front of her porch wearing a tank top and shorts. A Weed Whacker rested on her shoulder. Her blue eyes sparkled.

"I guess I'm an adult now. Squee! I bought my first home!

"I have no clue what I'm doing, I've been doing some research. From what I've gathered, your landscaping sets the stage for your house. You want it to be neat and tidy, from your lawn to your trees to your shrubs. It should create a complete picture and shouldn't have one thing that pulls your attention away from that completeness

She held up the Weed Whacker. "Taming of the shrubberies. This is me, taking a whack at it!" She giggled. "I know, bad dad joke."

There were snatches of her mowing the grass on her ride-on mower, weed whacking so bad that she divotted the dirt.

"I thought this was self-explanatory," she said, then laughed hysterically. *"It looks like I cut someone's hair with clippers and forgot to put the guard on. Look at it! It's a good thing no one lives next door."* She panned the camera up to my house. It was run down, but nowhere near how bad it was when I bought it. *"Maybe I should go practice on Haunty's yard first,"* she said. She leaned in closer to the camera and whispered, *"No one lives there, so no one would notice or complain."*

I leaned back in the chair and took a drink from my

water bottle. There were more videos of her I could watch, but I couldn't get past the first one.

That was not the Kate I knew.

Where did that Kate go?

And was that Kate still somewhere?

10

KATE

I pretended to dust my blinds as an excuse to snoop.

Watching my neighbor clean his garage had become a favorite pastime of mine. The pile outside increased on a daily basis. What if he threw out something else of value? I kept vigilant with my giant, hot pink fluffy feather duster.

Today wasn't too exciting. I could hear the banging from inside, but not much was being thrown outside. I also saw, right at the edge of the garage, my shop vac. Did that mean I was going to get another visit from him today? I *harrumphed!* I sure hoped not.

I grabbed the remote, ready to mute it at a moment's notice if the knock did come on my door so I could pretend not to be home. But then a movement caught my eye.

Grant hopped in his car, and tore off, leaving a cloud of dust in his wake.

What was that about? I twisted sideways, leaning over the arm of the couch to get a better sight line.

Had something happened? Another water leak? The fact

that he didn't know how to shut off the water under the sink proved he wasn't Mr. Fix-It.

Or something else. Say, like, he sliced his hand open and had to rush to the hospital? Or he got bit by a snake. Or worse, by a rabid raccoon. Were there squatters in his garage? Maybe he was just hungry and needed some Subway.

What was going on?

Maybe I'd go peek and see what he was doing in there. Maybe I could figure out why he left in such a hurry.

No. I would resist.

I aimed the remote at the TV.

But, what if there were more hidden treasures in the garage?

I grabbed my trusty feather duster and leaned over the side of the sofa. The hot pink duster extended my reach, enabling me to bend down the blinds. Just one more peek. Even from here, I could tell most of that pile was junk. The garage was full of junk and the dresser had been the exception. Had to've been.

I turned back to the TV, duster still in my hand. Remote in my other hand, I clicked on the YouTube to get my daily dose of disgust. I started typing *Merry loves Christm*—but changed my mind and shut the TV off.

I twisted to look back at the window.

If he drove into town, and then back, it was at least a good twenty minutes, maybe thirty. Ten minutes to drive to town, ten minutes at wherever he was going, and ten minutes back.

I checked my watch. He'd been gone ten, maybe fifteen minutes. Maybe.

I could make it. I could do it.

Oh, why not.

Fluffy duster in hand, I got off the couch and poked my head out my front door. Glancing at the street, and seeing no cars, I rushed out of my house and ran across the yards, hurdling the low bush that marked the property line, I stumbled and biffed it. I popped up, looked around to make sure no one saw me.

Like, who? Seriously? Haunty?

I brushed off my knees to erase any trace of eagerness, propping myself up with my super feather duster, then took off again.

I arrived undetected at Haunty's garage. The main door was wide open. I slowed about five feet from the garage, just to be cautious. After all, something scared him. And I didn't want something freaky to jump out at me. I brandished my feather duster, accidentally brushing it into the overgrown honeysuckle. A burst of scent hit my nose. At least that was pleasant.

I took a deep breath and performed a "fencer's" jump in front of the door. "Ha ha!" I yelled, then realized my scare tactic was pretty stupid.

Nothing.

Nothing happened. There was nothing there.

Which was good. I mean, I didn't want to have to defend myself with a feather duster. Because I couldn't imagine it could do a whole lot of good.

My breath slowed and my adrenaline level dropped and I took stock of the situation.

Honestly, I was a little disappointed in my neighbor's progress. From what I could see, there wasn't much improvement than the last time I saw inside his garage. And it had a really funky smell.

Another window on the side had been uncovered, so it was lighter inside, but it was still dim enough that I hesitated. When I'd shut off the water in his house, I half-expected someone to jump out of the cabinet with a butcher knife when I looked underneath the sink. Who knew what was lurking inside the garage?

I stood at the threshold, still unwilling to breach that boundary. I looked down at my hand and realized I didn't need to breach anything. I had my handy, dandy duster. That extended!

Leaning forward, I used my super duster to poke around. I lifted a few piles of yellowed newspapers, which resulted in them tipping over. The box underneath was not taped, and I finagled a flap to lift up. Sadly, I wasn't fully able to get a good view from where I was. I needed to position myself better.

Was it worth it? My eyes scanned the contents of the garage. Maybe this was a waste of time. I was getting my super duster super dirty for nothing.

My breath caught.

But wait...could that be a drop cloth over a big round mirror? Like a mirror belonging to a matching vanity to go with my dresser??? It was out of reach of my feather duster. I stepped forward...

"What are you doing in here?" Grant asked.

"Mod Podge Man!" Crap! I got caught.

"Grant."

"Grant, that's right. I was, uh, just looking."

He looked skeptical. "Do you make it a habit of walking into other people's garages without their permission?"

"Do you make a habit of driving away with your garage door open?"

"I was letting the bats out."

"You have bats?" I hadn't noticed Haunty being a bat

cave, but sometimes bats were out at night. They ate mosquitos, so I didn't beat them off with my broom.

He chuckled and shifted his weight to the other foot. "You could say I was just airing it out. I hoped it would smell better when I returned. Or maybe someone, like you, would steal all the stuff."

I ignored the part where he equated me to a garage-stuff-stealer. "Where did you go?"

He shrugged and held up the plastic Home Depot bag. "I needed face masks for the dust."

"You weren't gone very long."

His eyebrow quirked. "You've been keeping track?"

"No," I said. *Deny, deny, deny*. I totally had, at first. But then I got distracted and lost track of time. "You realize you're practically inviting criminal activity."

"Says the lady I found in my garage. So why are you here anyways?" He nodded at my feather duster. "Come by to dust all my crap before I toss it?"

I pointed to the driveway. With my duster. "I actually came to grab my shop vac."

He winced. "I'm not quite done with it. Can I borrow it just a little longer?"

"I suppose."

"That's very kind of you. I guess I can't hold your snooping against you."

"Hey, your garage was open. It was practically inviting looky-loos."

There was an expectant look on his face. "And?"

"And what?"

"Are you a looky-loo?"

I shuddered. "No! Your garage scares me. Seriously. It's spooky in there. You just said you have bats."

"Oh, but I think it'd be more like an antiques wonderland to you."

Antiques wonderland? Was he trying to be witty? "You've lost me. What do you mean?"

"I found some more of that furniture you like."

My heart did a little *pitter-patter*. "More?" I asked, my eyes darting to that (possible) Waterfall vanity mirror under the sheet.

"Yeah. I found something that kind of looks like the dresser. Want to see?"

Did I want to see? He obviously didn't pay much attention the last time he dangled a piece of furniture in front of me.

"C'mon, I'll show you what I've got." Grant said. "It's back here." He shimmied this way and that way through the piles of stuff.

Normally I hated going into dark garages because they were filled with spiders and cobwebs and bats. I loved the fake ones—like Halloween decorations—but was a baby when it came to the real deal. Obviously, the pull of antique furniture was stronger than my hate of spiders and bats in dark, scary, dank places.

I took a deep breath, held my feather duster close in case I needed to ward off any marauding spiders or beat off any bats, and followed him in. After some shuffling, I met him in front of a beautiful, if worn, wardrobe with a mirror inset. He wiped his hand across the front, clearing the dust into a "V" pattern. "The mirror is cracked, but other than that it seems to be intact. But I'm not the expert who's able to assess the shape of this furniture."

My lungs felt like they were about to burst. It was! My breath rushed out. "Once we get it outside in the sunlight, we can tell better," I said, anxious to get a good look at it.

He dragged a few boxes outside, clearing a wider path for us and uncovering another window in the process. Light flooded in, making it easier to see the furniture, but also the amount of stuff still jammed inside the garage. It wasn't encouraging.

"Here, help me with this, please," he said.

I grabbed one side and he grabbed the other side and tipped it toward himself. Then we walked it out carefully. Once we passed the threshold of the garage, we set it down to examine it closer.

The patina of its wood shone in the bright midday sun. It wasn't perfect, of course. There were chips in the veneer, but the Herringbone pattern was unmistakable. The hardware on the five drawers were perfect, no chips or broken pieces. I dusted it with my super duster, creating a cloud of dust in the air, but exposing the deep brown tones of the wood better.

I wanted to hug it. I literally wanted to wrap my arms around the beautiful piece and thank it for its existence. But that would be weird to someone who did not understand the value of what he uncovered, nor the beauty of it.

Instead of hugging it, I pattered my hands together in delight. "You're right, this goes with the dresser!" I'd suspected it, but the matching Bakelite hardware and patterns of chevron wood inlay confirmed it.

I turned and looked back in the garage. With critical eyes, I scanned the mounds, piles and corners of the room. I had to get my hands on whatever was under that drop cloth. And was that the edge of a headboard? "There might be more back there."

"Do you want this, too?" he said.

I bounced my feather duster against my crossed arm. "This is collectible furniture. It might be worth upwards of a thousand dollars." I watched him, waiting for the offer to be withdrawn.

"I don't care," he said. "I don't want it and you do. You were practically drooling from the window the other day."

Was I really so transparent? I wiped the side of my mouth to make sure I really wasn't salivating now. There wasn't any spit to be found.

"And you practically fondled the dresser."

I quickly removed my hand from where I had been resting it on the curved side.

"I was *not* fondling the dresser!"

He waved away my excuse. "Whatever. Consider it all a gift."

I had to rein in my grin. "Really?"

"When was the last time you got a gift?" he asked.

I didn't even know. Christmas, maybe? I shrugged.

"All you have to do is say 'thank you' and not argue."

"Okay." I nodded. "Thank you."

In order to move past the uncomfortable moment, I took a closer look at the wardrobe piece. I opened the drawers to see how they glided. I tested the door, checking the hinges and if the magnetic closure worked. It wasn't in pristine condition but I loved it anyway.

"Oh, and hey," he called from inside the garage again. "I think you're right. There might be one more piece. A desk. Here, come see."

I returned to the back of the garage and found him uncovering the round mirror from off the vanity. I was right. There was also a headboard (I thought so!) and footboard leaning against the same wall nearby. After carrying them out, I whistled softly. "This is gorgeous," I said. "I can't believe you have a full bedroom set in your garage and you were just going to throw it out."

If the Broom Fits

"I wish it was a classic Camaro instead. You're really passionate about furniture, aren't you?"

"I am. Or I was." I quickly corrected.

"What do you mean you were? You're not anymore? Because it seems to me like you're pretty excited about this furniture."

"I used to be in the business, I guess you could say. But it's been a while." I continued with my inspection, hoping he would let me concentrate and so I could avoid more questions.

"You're taking it, right? That would be great because it'd be one less thing I'd have to throw away." He rubbed his hands together then wiped them on the front of his jeans.

I looked up from my inspection. "You sure?"

"I'm so sure I'll help you carry it to your house. Or you can wait until the next time Bill comes and he could give us a hand."

"I think you and I can handle it." I wanted to hurry and get out of there. I didn't want to wait for Bill to help. I didn't feel like making small talk with Bill and hearing how his life was moving along and mine wasn't.

It took a couple of precarious trips with the hand truck, but we did it. Everything fit neatly inside my garage.

"Thanks for your help and for the furniture. That was incredibly generous," I said as I put the door down.

"Glad it's found a good home." He smiled.

Maybe he would be an okay neighbor.

11

KATE

On a high from my newly gifted furniture, I thought about what to do with it. And where to put it. The answer was obvious. One of my spare rooms. But then I'd have to deal with the spare rooms. That was not something I could deal with today.

And, if I was going to do something with them, say, paint them, I'd have to face the She Shed again.

The idea of it made me sink into the sofa. I'd been avoiding it for a while now. Actually, *more* than just a while.

But I couldn't just leave the bedroom set in the garage. Eventually I'd have to park in there again, *sooo...*

I stood up, stepped into the hall that gave me a clear view out my kitchen window. There she stood. My She Shed. It didn't have to be a long visit. And heck, I survived the last visit. Bats and birds didn't attack me when I ran in, so I knew my workshop hadn't become a cave or a nest. Ghosts of days gone by couldn't haunt me if I didn't stay too long. I could scrape up a little bit of bravery.

Without further thought, so I couldn't talk myself out of it, I marched out my back door.

My workshop loomed in front of me.

For the second time in nearly three years, I grasped the round door knob on the lavender door and entered. I turned on the lights. It smelled like dust. Dust particles floated in front of the windows. Dust was everywhere. I traced my name with a finger on the table closest to me and grumbled to myself. I'd have to clean everything. But I couldn't be dissuaded by a little housekeeping. I had to get that furniture out of the garage and get my car back in. I opened the windows to let the dust escape.

I hit the seat of my teal faux-fur spinning desk chair to dispel the dust, then sat in it and rolled back until I was almost against the wall and took stock of the space.

A tarp was still on the floor, brushes, scattered around, a couple dried with paint.

I examined my paint sprayer and wondered if it still worked. Luckily, it had been cleaned after the last time I used it, but I didn't know if there were seals that might've dried out for lack of use.

Old newspaper, yellowed and dry with age, covered one work table. I used my feet to kick it off the table and into the trash bucket beside it. It wasn't a huge mess, since I had usually kept my workspace tidy and the need to clean was more from lack of attention than just being a slob.

Okay, see, that wasn't so scary. It was just a work area. Literally just work. Nothing more. Working here was just like having a second job.

I would return, with my trusty duster in hand, and I would fix this place up and clear out the cobwebs.

12

GRANT

I did a perimeter check around my property first thing in the morning in a futile attempt to find Midnight. The dumpsters were being delivered today and I was sure that noise would scare her.

I had to find her, but where was she? My eyes wandered across the yard to Kate's house. Did Midnight ever go over there? I mean, if she had a choice, wouldn't she choose the house that smelled better? I would.

It only took a minute or two to cross the yard and once again, I was at the familiar lavender door. I wouldn't be surprised if one of these times she pointed out how needy I was. Not the thing I'd want pointed out.

She opened the door, an irritated look on her face.

"Hey, sorry for the inconvenience, but have you seen my cat around?"

She squinted. "You have a cat."

"Yes, and she's lost."

Kate shook her head. "I haven't."

I sighed. "Alright. If you see her, will you text me? She's all black. Her name is Midnight."

She lifted her shoulder slightly. "Sure. I guess." She pulled her phone out of her raggedy bathrobe pocket. "What's your number?"

Kate punched in the information on her phone as I recited it. "Thanks," I said. At least now I had another pair of eyes watching for Midnight.

"Yup," she said, then immediately closed her door.

I had just stepped off her porch when Bill roared up in his truck.

He climbed down from his truck and walked over.

"Hey, hey. I see you met your neighbor, Kate," Bill said.

"Yeah, I have."

He put his hands on his hips and stared at her house. "I'm surprised she's talking to you." Bill put his hands on his hips and stared at her house.

Now I was curious what her deal was. "Why?" Did she hate the last neighbors? Maim them? Kill them?

Bill faced me and shook his head. "Not just the last neighbors. Everyone in the whole town."

"She seemed nice enough when I originally met her at the hobby store." Again, she wasn't the welcome wagon, but she didn't chase me down with a shot gun, either.

He chuckled a little. "Yeah. Well, if you're rude at work you get fired. Outside of work she's kind of known as the town witch."

I looked at her house and then back at Bill. "The town witch? Like with the cauldron and a book of spells?" Did she cast spells and make voodoo dolls? She didn't seem freaky. Didn't walk around all in black. I didn't see pentagrams hanging on her walls or wind chimes made out of dried, human bones. At least I didn't think I had. I hadn't seen her whole backyard in the daylight. Was there a huge cauldron or a wood-burning stove I hadn't noticed?

Bill seemed amused at my concern. "No, not that kind of witch-witch but like a witchy person." Bill seemed amused at my concern.

"Well, yeah, I can see that. She's a bit abrasive at first, but she's also been pretty helpful. Why do people call her a witch?"

"She's mean. She wasn't like that in high school. She was actually friendly back then. Now, she just seems to ignore people, like she's avoiding them. One time I ran into her at the grocery store and said "hello". She nodded and kept going. Which is weird because we used to hang out with the same group of friends in high school."

"She answered the times I knocked on her door."

His eyes widened. "You've knocked on her door?" His eyes widened a little bit.

"Well, yeah. I had water spilling all over the place and needed help shutting off the water valve, so I ran over there." I left out the attempt at trying to apologize. I didn't want to talk about that. "She was very capable of taking care of it. More capable than me." I sounded more and more sexist as I told the story.

"I'm surprised she helped."

Why? I wanted to know more. "What happened to her?"

He shook his head. "I dunno. She went out of state to college and returned home a couple of years later. She dated a guy who was on the local news, Sean something, and they got engaged and then broke up."

"I see."

"It was kind of a public thing. After that she changed. She put on a lot of weight too."

I wasn't going to touch that. Mira hated talking about her weight.

"That's when the town witch thing started," Bill added.

"Sounds like she was a nice person before."

"Nice enough." He shrugged, then said, "Nice enough that she didn't have a reputation."

"She became very nice when I gave her some old furniture I found in the garage," I said. "Kind of went nuts over it, in fact."

"Hey! Got any more to give her? Sounds like you're getting a glimpse of the old Kate."

"She'll eventually warm up, I figure," I said. I wanted to be on good terms with my neighbor. Maybe she just needed some ice cream or cookies or more vintage furniture. Maybe my attic had something good in it. I'd been afraid to check it out.

"Don't let your guard down, dude. You haven't known Kate long enough. It generally doesn't matter how nice you treat her; she isn't nice back. You know what they say, if the broom fits."

"What? Use it? Sweep with it?"

"Ride it. Meaning she didn't get that reputation for no reason." Bill sounded honest, not malicious.

"Kate doesn't seem like a bad person. Grumpy doesn't equate bad." I should give her the benefit of the doubt, until she showed me otherwise.

"She's certainly not the Queen of Friendliness," Bill said.

I shook my head. "I firmly believe that she could be nice all of the time. She just has to be treated right. If you treat a girl like queen she's going to act like a queen."

Bill laughed. "Good luck with that, dude."

AUGUST

13

KATE

"Are you trying to die?" I yelled at Grant. I had just driven up my driveway, saw him in his backyard and scrambled out of the car as quickly as I could. Over the last couple of weeks, I had plenty of chances to watch the progression or the house. Dumpsters had been delivered, windows replaced, the roof had been repaired, electricians and plumbers had come and gone, appliances had been delivered. But those had been professionals.

Clearly, he didn't know what he was doing because this stunt was downright dangerous.

He was perched on the top of the ladder, as in the very top, where it warns you not to stand, with a chain saw in his hands. There was a large tree limb before him, about twelve inches in diameter, and I was pretty sure he was about to cut it off the tree.

"No," he said, and lowered the chainsaw.

I could smell the exhaust. Had he been at this very long or had I arrived just in time?

"Well, there's a good chance you will if you continue."

"You mean trimming the tree?"

I pointed to the branch I suspected he was about to "trim". "Trim or cut?"

"Cut."

"Standing on that ladder? It seriously looks like it is about to collapse." The ladder was wooden and even without being up close, I could see it was wobbly.

"It's the only one I've got." He shrugged, as if that justified his poor judgement.

"Did you bring it with you?"

"I got it out of my garage. The last people left it."

I pointed at his garage. "Nothing good has come from that garage except the furniture you gave me."

His eyes met mine. "Do you have a better idea?"

"Yes. I'll lend you my ladder and you'll be safer. But, before I do that, I have to ask if you have ever used a chainsaw."

"I haven't, but how hard could it be?" He shrugged again.

Oh, boy. Did he not understand how dangerous this whole thing was? A chainsaw. An old ladder. "Please promise me you'll research it first before you attempt this. I can't stand by and watch as you accidently kill yourself."

"I doubt that will happen."

I pointed directly at him. "Better yet, hire someone. You'll thank me. Besides, I already called the cops out here once, don't make me call an ambulance next." It wasn't like I wanted to play some weird Emergency Response/911 Bingo.

He seemed resigned as he carefully climbed down the ladder, chainsaw in hand. "All right. But I don't see why you're freaking out."

"Chainsaw kickback, it's a real thing. The tree limb could split, throw you off balance and tip over the ladder. Chainsaw injuries are nothing to joke about."

"Okay, okay," he said, his voice full of resignation. "I'll call Bill."

∽

Grant's cat stared at me from the porch. At least, I assumed it was Midnight, since she was black. Ever since he stopped by looking for her, I'd been putting a little food and water out on my back porch and the food was usually gone. But I had yet to see her until today.

I went to the cupboard and grabbed a small bag of Tuna-flavored Temptations and lowered myself into sitting position on my kitchen floor close to my open back door. "Well, hello there, little one. Nice to meet you. Want to come in? I have treats." I shook the bag gently.

"Meow," she said, but didn't move.

I waited for her to approach.

She didn't look particularly scared or skittish, she just sat there, eyeing me with her wide, green eyes. I reached my arm out, slowly, trying to entice her to come to me. She regarded my hand, made no attempt to acknowledge it beyond that.

"You came to me, kitty. The least you can do is to make an effort to be friends," I said. But, then again, this was a cat I was talking to. Cats did whatever they pleased, whenever they pleased and however they pleased.

I put a couple of treats in a row, leading into the house, seeing if that would work. She sniffed at them. When she was just about to step inside, there was a knock on the front door. I glanced at the door and then at the cat, but she was gone.

Oh! So close!

I climbed off the floor, brushed myself off and went to the opposite door. It had to be Grant. It was always Grant.

Without bothering to check the peephole, I opened the door. "You ruined it," I said, then held up my thumb and index finger about an inch apart from each other. "I was about this close to getting Midnight in my house."

Grant held up two flat boxes.

Gramaldo's Pizza. Yum. My mouth watered.

"You saw her?" he said.

I nodded.

His chest visibly decompressed. "She's alive!" he cried. "Hold this and I'm going to try and catch her." He handed the pizza to me and ran off to the backyard.

After setting the pizza down, I followed him out. Two was better than one when searching for a pet.

"She comes by every morning and every evening, so I feed her."

"I'd come every morning and night if you fed me, too," he said.

Exactly what I'm afraid of.

"I put food out in my house and it does get eaten, I just don't see her. I don't know how she's getting in or out, or where's she's hiding, but I feel better knowing you've seen her in person," he said.

"She's a beauty," I said.

His concern for the cat was obvious, but after ten minutes of searching, my concern for the food going cold took priority. We went back inside to the kitchen.

I pointed at the boxes. "What's with the pizza?" I asked.

"I didn't know what you like to drink so I brought pizza instead."

"How do you know what kind of pizza I like?" I challenged. I generally liked anything with cheese on it and wasn't particular about pizza toppings, except for eggs. Eggs didn't belong on pizza.

"I don't," he said. "I gambled on pepperoni and cheese."

"What if I'm vegan?" I asked.

"Then I should've bought cauliflower pizza. Are you?"

"No."

"So, you like cheese pizza?" he asked.

"Yup." Secretly, I was thrilled at the prospect of dinner being delivered, without any effort on my part.

"I figured you could supply your own drinks."

He had planned this enough to make assumptions about toppings and drinks. "Now why are you here again, but with pizza?"

"I owe you." he said.

Owe me? "For what?"

I didn't want him owe me anything. But then he did things, like giving me that dresser, and then giving a whole bedroom set. If anything, *I* owed *him*.

"You spared me from death by chainsaw," he said. "And you've been feeding my lost cat."

I folded my arms and shook my head. "Still even."

"If we're even, then we can sit down and enjoy a pizza as neighbors." He shifted his weight from one foot to another. Was he nervous?

I wasn't looking for company for the evening, but the scent of the pizza weakened my resolve. My stomach grumbled. I was grumpy but not a complete jerk.

"Since you've never really said where your wife is, I need to make sure you're single."

I wanted to be clear. I wasn't into married men.

"I am. But this isn't a date," he said.

With that, I motioned for him to take a seat. "I didn't

think it was." I didn't feel like he was hitting on me. It wasn't even close to flirting.

He pulled out a chair and sat. "So, you agree that we can have pizza together?"

"I wasn't planning on agreeing, but I guess you're kind of twisting my words around so that it sounds like we're agreeing." I gathered paper plates, napkins and set them on the table. One on each end.

"Is that a yes?"

It seemed like he was more insistent on clarifying this point more than I was. "A reluctant 'yes'."

He smiled. "I'll take a reluctant 'yes' over an adamant 'no'."

"Why do you keep coming over here? We're not friends." I grabbed a slice of pizza. The cheese stretched across the table from the box to my plate. We might not have been friends, but I was willing to eat the pizza he brought tonight.

"But we're neighbors who could be friends once we get to know each other."

I snickered. Was that his goal?

"Besides, you saved my life today."

I stopped mid-bite. "You checked out how to cut a tree?"

"Yes." He nodded. "You were right. I probably would've injured myself. I also turned the job over to Bill."

"See. I'm impressed." I made a sweeping motion with my hand. "You took advice and are still alive because of it. Are you also a man who asks directions?"

He laughed. "I am."

That wasn't a bad quality in a man.

14

GRANT

Deciding to get a jump on the next day, and having nothing better to do in my life, I attempted to scrape the hallway ceiling. It wasn't easy. In fact, it was downright tedious. After giving it a go for five minutes, I didn't have the energy or motivation to push through the task. I cursed the popcorn finish. It mocked my pain, as did the truth. I was an idiot thinking I could take on a project like this and actually finish it.

I'd have to save that nightmare project for another day.

Instead, I took a shower and went to Kate's.

Kate didn't open the lavender door all the way. Instead, she rested against it, her hand on the knob. "Can't stay away from my magnetic personality, or are you just here for the A/C?"

"More for the second, some of the first." I smiled and waited to see if I'd get a reaction. I was rewarded with a hint of a smile and an invitation inside. "Actually, I just realized, I really need help."

This time she did smile. "Like professional help?"

"I probably should get evaluated, thinking it would be a good idea to take on this project. And that's why I'm turning to you."

"I am not a trained professional in psychiatry or construction. But if you need an armchair psychiatrist, my sister, Chrissy, loves to tell it like it is. And if you need a professional contractor, I'm not your girl."

I looked around the room, reminding myself that she had done all this. I'd seen it on her YouTube channel. I knew she was capable. More capable than me. "I just need help."

She crossed her arms, looking wary. "What're you thinking?"

"I don't know what I'm doing and I'm in way over my head and I need you."

"The words every girl wants to hear: I need you."

Was she flirting now?

Her comment threw me and I opened my mouth to speak, but didn't know what to say.

She checked her watch, then motioned with her head toward my house. "C'mon. Why don't you show me?"

There was a quiet scratching on her back door in the kitchen. "Do you hear that?" I asked. "Could it be Midnight?"

I felt better knowing Midnight came to Kate's, even if it was only occasionally. I worried less about the nights she didn't come home. At least she wasn't out wandering the woods. But it was supposed to storm tonight and I wanted her home. Midnight had been Mira's cat. She always preferred my wife and tolerated me. After Mira's passing, Midnight's affection for me hadn't grown by much. Despite Midnight's affection, or lack of affection, for me, I still liked having her around. In a way, she was all I had left of Mira.

"Maybe. She was just here."

I pointed toward the sound. "Should we check?" The sun had set while I had been here. Dusk was still light enough to see. Better to see now than to make a second attempt with the flashlight. "Thunder scares her and I want her to be safe."

She nodded emphatically. "Absolutely. That poor baby. We don't want her out in the storm."

She turned and I followed, catching a whiff of her laundry detergent again. I actually looked forward to the day when my house could smell like laundry detergent or dryer sheets or anything other than a musty, old cellar.

"Either that or it's wild animals. I think I had raccoons at the house last night," I said. It was annoying and inconvenient. They woke me from a dead sleep just after 3 a.m. and I couldn't get back to sleep.

"Raccoons?" Her voice lifted in surprise. "They'll wander out of the woods, especially if they smell food. You don't feed them, do you?"

I shook my head. "Nope. I only want one pet, and that's Midnight."

The scratching came again.

"And hopefully that's her," I said.

We walked to her back door and as soon as she opened it, Midnight zoomed in and was down the hall before I realized what happened.

We spent a few minutes calling her and Kate checked under her bed, but only in one room. The other two doors were shut, so Midnight didn't go in there. After checking everywhere we could, she was nowhere to be found. Felt like déjà vu from my first day, but at Kate's house.

"She might just be freaked out. Why don't we let her

calm down while we check out your house? She'll come out when she's ready," Kate said.

We tromped across the yards and into my house. Inside, I flipped the light switch and dim light lit up the living room.

She looked around and then cleared her throat. "What exactly you need help with? I mean, besides everything?"

I pointed my index finger up. "It's those popcorn ceilings. I'm not having much luck." I knew she knew how to do them—she'd done a YouTube video on it.

"Can't Bill help? Or do you just need to borrow my ladder? If that's the case, you didn't have to drag me over here. You could've just asked."

I felt stupid and weak. It would be great if I could manage all of these projects myself, but I couldn't. Wasn't that a sign of strength? Me asking for help? "Well, yeah, Bill helps on some things. But paying him by the hour is getting expensive. And I've had to hire some real professionals since I've acknowledged that sometimes it better to leave it to the professionals." I sounded like a Home Depot ad.

She snickered. "You want free labor? That's not going to happen."

I was prepared with an offer going into this conversation. "I could pay you something, just less than Bill. I'd have to look at my budget."

She cocked her head. "How do you even have money? Do you work? I don't even know what you do if you work. Are you independently wealthy?"

It was my turn to laugh. "If I was independently wealthy, I would've hired people to renovate it for me. I'm a high school teacher. Just taking a year off."

She scratched her head. "That doesn't make that much

money, does it? I mean, that you can just take off work for a year to fix a house."

I didn't add the key information: the insurance money. "And some decent savings."

"So, really, your budget is cheap-to-free," she said.

"Not exactly, but something like that. I'm trying to put in as much sweat equity as I can."

"Because you can't afford a real professional."

"Well, so far you've been able to fix all my fixer-upper stuff. You know, you're kind of like Bill, but female."

"Ha ha. Maybe even better than Bill."

"Definitely better-looking."

Her eyes darted over to me and then quickly away. "I wouldn't say I'm an expert. It was a hobby a while back, but I definitely know what my limits are and when I need to contract out. Popcorn ceilings, that's pretty easy. Electrical and plumbing, not so much."

"I tried YouTube, cut you're more fun. I propose a work-for-trade."

"A trade? What are you thinking and what am I agreeing to?

"I'll mow your lawn for the rest of the season, if you'll help me scrape my ceilings."

She looked over her shoulder as if she was mentally measuring the size of her lawn. "I have a ride-on mower, so it's not a lot of work."

Riding on a lawn mower versus scraping these ceilings alone. The answer was a no-brainer. "Just think of the summer days with high humidity. It would be one less hot, sweaty chore you'd have to do." Why was I working so hard to convince her? Just listening to myself, I was basically begging her to do an outside job in the hot summer. But that wasn't it. It was nice to have company. Her company.

"Okay," she said. "I'll do it in exchange for mowing my lawn. We can start tomorrow night."

"It's a deal."

"But," she held up my index finger, "I'll require pizza."

15

GRANT

The good (and probably only) thing about living in a house while reno-ing it was I didn't feel obligated to clean up before Kate came over. My house was always a mess. I used her shop vac to quickly suck up the obvious dust and called it good.

Kate arrived, dressed to work in a faded tank top, cut-offs and work boots. Her hair was pulled up in a ponytail. It was a good look on her.

"Midnight finally came out of hiding. I found her sleeping in a small basket under my TV stand this afternoon. She was way too cute to wake up."

"Glad she appeared," I said.

"Maybe she should stay at my place until your reno's done."

It made sense, even though I hated to admit it. "Yeah. Sounds scare her and I'm sure she can't stand the smell."

"Don't worry, she'll be fine. It's safer than letting her roam around outside."

She was right. "As long as you're okay with it." I had to think about the best interest of Midnight.

Kate sniffed the air.

Crap! Did it still stink in here? I sniffed the air also.

"No pizza?" she asked.

"Not yet," I said. "I wasn't sure if you'd be hungry right away."

"I'm always hungry. And let's be honest, popcorn ceilings are a big ask. I'm doing it for the pizza."

"But with the added bonus of me mowing your lawn," I said.

She made a snorting noise. "With an added bonus that I have a ride-on mower, so it practically does the work for you."

She walked in to the front room and looked up. "This the room of choice?"

"Yes," I said. "How exactly does someone scrape popcorn ceilings? Can I use a vacuum?"

Her eyes widened. "You haven't tried that already, have you?"

I laughed.

"Please tell me the picture of you standing on your rickety ladder, with my shop vac hose stretched as far as it could go, scraping it across the ceiling has not actually happened."

I shook my head. "No, but I've seriously considered it. I thought about getting a head start before you came over tonight, thinking maybe we could get it done in a night."

It was her turn to shake her head. "Doubtful. It's a process. If you spray it with water and let it soften for a few minutes and then scrape it with a paint scraper, it comes off pretty well."

"So, spray it with a hose?"

"No."

"We could give it a try." I was only half-joking. Mostly, I

was desperate. I wanted this done. Actually, I needed it done because the drywallers were coming next week and I didn't want them back a second time to do the ceilings.

Another head shake. This one more emphatic. "Not the hose. You'll just end up with another flood and water damage."

"True."

She wagged her finger at me. "Let me put it this way, you try funny stuff with that ceiling and my shop vac and I'll put it on your tab."

I waved my hands in surrender. "Okay, okay, *fine*. We'll do it your way," I joked.

She scanned the room. "Do you have paint scrapers? It would definitely go easier if you have the right supplies.

"I'd want something wider, like a snow plow. Take care of it in one fell swoop."

"That's called a front loader and that will take care of more than just your ceiling problem."

I pictured the ceiling falling down around. "Yeah, right. I'm trying to repair and not destroy."

"Exactly," she said. "So, back to the paint scraper. You have one?"

I dropped his head a little and had a bashful expression. "No."

"How about a spray bottle?"

The expression remained. "No," I said.

"How about a ladder? Have you bought a ladder yet? A tarp? A face mask?"

"I have a face mask."

"I'm talking construction ones, not just those blue things you used when you cleaned out the garage. You don't want to inhale that stuff."

"Oh, look at you. Caring about me. It's cute." I elbowed her gently in the arm.

"Tease all you want. It won't be funny if you get sick from inhaling it. You know, cancer, tuberculosis, mesothelioma."

I shivered. "I'm pretty sure I won't get tuberculosis from scraping the ceiling. The other two, I'm not so sure."

"What *do* you have?" She seemed exasperated, but she always seemed like that.

I held up my arms. "Nothing but these."

She shook her head slowly. "Basically, you have no supplies."

"Except my arms."

She inhaled deeply. "Let's go see what I have in my garage. You might need to make a trip to Home Depot."

I smiled broadly. "The words every man wants to hear."

"And how about you order up that pizza too? Delivery takes forever out here."

I followed her back to her garage and ordered the pizza on my cell phone while she rummaged around inside. Since we had shared several pizzas, I didn't bother asking her about toppings. I went ahead with the usuals.

Holding an orange five-gallon bucket, she murmured to herself as she selected stuff from the shelves. "Putty knife...sponge...sanding block."

I had another wave of garage envy as I admired her organization. Someday, my garage would look like hers. I couldn't wait.

She grabbed a container like what I'd seen the Orkin guy use.

"Is that to spray pest control?" I asked.

She looked at it, and then handed it to me. "No. It's to spray water. Don't worry, it's clean."

Who was I to argue? "Don't worry. I trust you."

She threw an extra pair of goggles and a plastic drop cloth in, and pointed to the ladder. "If you can grab that, I think we're good."

～

After pizza, we got to work. She sprayed the ceiling with water and I scraped.

When we finished the living room, I stretched my arms then let them drop by my side. They ached from working above my head. I looked at my watch; it had only been an hour.

"Ready to take a break?" I asked.

"Yes." She rolled her shoulders. "I'm going to pay for my kindness tomorrow with sore muscles."

We sat in the Adirondack chairs, currently in the kitchen and drank raspberry lemonade from red Solo cups.

"How about we make our scraping party a little more interesting?" I asked.

She drained her cup. "How? By being done for the night?

"No, by playing a game."

Her eyes narrowed suspiciously. "What game?"

"I ask you a question—"

She cut in. "Twenty questions? Nope, not a fan."

I held up my index finger "Not twenty. One. And in return, you ask me a question." She had asked how I was funding the house reno, so I could delve into her private life a little. If she went for it.

She squinted at me quizzically. "You can't be that interesting."

"You'll never know unless you play."

She rolled her eyes.

I pulled out my bribery card. "I have ice cream for you ice cream."

She considered it for a couple of seconds. "Okay, I'll do it."

I grabbed two single-serve ice cream containers of rocky road from my freezer, purchased especially with her in mind, and two plastic spoons. I handed her one and then sat back down.

"How did you learn how to do this kind of stuff?"

"Trial and error. Lots of error," she said, then took a bite.

"What made you want to do it?"

Mira. She wanted to do it. This was all her idea. "HGTV," I said.

She giggled.

"What?" I asked.

"Somehow I can't picture you lounging around watching HGTV."

I pointed at her with my white, plastic spoon. "It's not just for women. That's the Lifetime channel." Actually, I never really watched HGTV with Mira. Now I wished I had.

"Do you watch that, too?" she asked.

"For the record, no. But enough about me. It's my turn," I said. "Tell me about your YouTube channel."

"Ooooh," She made an exaggerated O-shape with her lips. "So, these are going to be *personal* questions, not just stuff like what flavor of ice cream I'd like to have, or what's my favorite color?"

"Deeply personal questions. Deep."

Would she answer?

She thought for a moment.

Maybe she needed some encouragement, although I was doubtful it would sway her. But it was worth a try. "I've seen a couple of them. You were good."

Her neck straightened minutely. What seemed like longer than a few seconds, she gave a small shrug.

"I started it on a whim. I already had a blog, but then I recorded my first attempt at a home improvement project, which was a complete fail, and it sort of just took off. Then I decorated it for Halloween and it went viral."

"I see." I hadn't gotten to the Halloween stuff yet.

She scraped some ice cream from the side of the carton and ate it.

"My turn?" she asked.

I nodded.

"You've mentioned you had a wife. Where is she?" She stopped "What I mean—"

"You, uh..." I stuttered, then cleared my throat. I should've expected that question. "You make it sound like she was killed and her body was never found and I'm the number one suspect."

"If I thought that, I wouldn't be alone with you and tools."

"She passed away two and a half years ago."

The familiar look of pity crossed her face. She stopped scraping her ice cream container. "I'm sorry," she said. "What happened?"

"She was diagnosed with cancer and four months later she was gone." It still managed to catch in my throat.

She touched my arm briefly. "Oh, wow. I'm so sorry."

I motioned around the room. "This was her dream, so here I am living it. It just took longer than we both thought."

There was an uncomfortable pause. I checked to see if I had missed any nuts in my ice cream.

"I understand. Unfortunately, there isn't a perfect timeline for getting over your grief. Or so they tell me."

"When Mira died it felt like people just expected me to

bounce back after a certain amount of time. They had moved on with their lives but I hadn't."

"Exactly. It's like part of you has died. Literally, for you," she said. She spoke slowly, as if choosing her words carefully. "I haven't experienced death like that."

The air was heavy for a few seconds.

We ate in silence for a minute or two before I started with more questions. I didn't want to dwell on Mira. "What changed your trajectory in life? It seemed like the YouTube gig was going well."

Kate chewed on the corner of her lip, before offering a half smile. "It's not as painful or profound as yours."

I shook my head. "We're not trying to one-up each other's pain. I just want to know."

"My fiancé didn't show up for our wedding. Totally blindsided me."

"What a loser," I said.

"Definitely a loser. And a coward. Turns out he'd been cheating on me and just"—she made air quotes—"didn't know how to tell me."

Ouch. "I see why you're bitter," I said. "Are you over your ex?"

"I despise him."

"Understandably, but are you over him?"

"Definitely," she said without hesitation. "But there was some collateral damage to him dissing me at the altar."

"What's worse than that?"

"I had sponsors for the wedding. They canceled their sponsorship. I got sued for breach of contract and I was completely humiliated."

A woman scorned. I understood her just a little bit more. "He hit you with a low blow emotionally and financially. Someone needs to face punch him."

"Right! That's what I thought. But I was already dealing with a disaster." She laughed bitterly. "I couldn't face the public. People are horrible on social media. And I certainly couldn't run him over with my car. Something like that would get filmed and go viral. So, I just stopped. I walked away."

Bill's story about the public break-up echoed in my mind. "Seems like you were you doing well at it."

There was another bitter laugh. "I paid off my house just with affiliate income."

"Then your life got nuked."

"Yup, pretty much. In one crappy, sucky, no-good, terrible day," she said. "But look at me, helping renovate a house again." She offered a pained smile.

I flashed her a smile. "I feel special."

She pointed her spoon at me. "You should. I don't make that exception for just anybody. But it's looking better."

"It still looks like a dump."

"Your house is a dump—"

"Thank you," I interrupted. "You are so kind."

She held her hand up to stop me from talking. "Let me finish," she said with a smile. "I was thinking about it."

"You were thinking about me?"

"About your house," she said.

"Which means about me." I smiled widely. I took a bite of ice cream while maintaining eye contact with her.

"Your house has a ton of potential."

I licked my spoon, then held it up and used it to point around the room. "I don't see any of it. I'm just ready for it to be done so I can stop living in a construction zone.

"It will. It just takes time."

I was slightly more motivated from her pep talk. "Think we can finish these ceilings tomorrow night?"

She leaned forward. "It'll cost you."

"Name your price." I really wanted to be done with this job. And I liked having her company.

"Pizza and ice cream," she said.

"Done," I said, with no hesitation.

16

KATE

Today was the day. I would face the She Shed. Armed with my duster, I stepped in, noticing I breathed a little easier this time. It still smelled dusty, but that would be taken care of when I was through. I stood in the doorway and scanned the space.

Mentally I made a list of what I needed to do, and then went about it in an orderly fashion.

I sprayed, I wiped, I moved, I vacuumed, and got it all done. Once everything was wiped down, I plugged in the mini fridge in the corner, then sat down on the red velvet couch and took in the space. I was sweaty and my hands smelled like wet dust, but my She Shed was pretty again.

And now I could start on the bedroom set. Nervous energy gripped my stomach. This was exciting.

But first, Home Depot.

⁓

THE DISTINCT SMELL OF HOME DEPOT HIT MY NOSE AS I stepped through the automatic doors. It was a weird combination of fertilizer, rubber and paint. It wasn't my favorite smell in the world; I preferred the scent of freshly mixed paint. But it still smelled comforting.

Hello, Home Depot, my old friend.

I went straight over to the paint department and stared at the array of paint chips. It was sadly ironic that I was buying paint, because just four years before, I had been approached by a company to have my own paint line called Kate Paints. It would've only been distributed through craft stores or smaller independent distributors, but still. It would've been nationally available. It got put on the back burner temporarily while I planned my wedding. Then everything fell apart, and things temporarily set aside got permanently set aside and almost forgotten. Like my paint line.

The display was so colorful, perfect, happy, as if beckoning me to try each one. I tended to be a gray person. Paint everything gray and add a splash of color (usually purple or orange—more purple these days) in other ways through details. But my favorite color combination was gray and purple.

The problem with paint chips was the color always looked great on a small chip, but once put on a bigger surface, say, a bedframe or a wall, you noticed things you didn't notice before. The color had a little too much grey in it, or yellow. The white looked dirty instead of clean. The tan looked like mud instead of light brown. Or even worse, poop. Once you saw the bigger picture, that perfect color on that little sample square lied to you. It was completely different than what you thought you were getting. And you realize it wasn't really exactly what you wanted. With some colors, you knew right away, and with others, you needed to try it out for a while to make sure you actually knew. And others, you keep hoping it will be right. That once the paint dries, it will look like more of what you imagined. That once you put more on, paint a bigger area, it will look better. That maybe once it's been on the wall for a while, it will grow on you, or you will decide that it *is* right.

But what I'd learned from relationships and paint, was that if you're not feeling it, you might need to consider going a different direction.

Which led me back to my favorite color for furniture: gray. Gray was safe. Gray was dependable. Gray went with anything. Gray was basic and neutral and didn't cause problems. I decided I needed more gray in my life.

But then a bold teal caught my eye. *What if?* Came to mind. The thought caught me by surprise. Did I dare? It wasn't my usual color combination, but it would work.

I waffled. It'd be easier to paint a wall a bold color than a whole bedroom set. That way, it'd be easier to paint over if I decided the color was not for me. Furniture was more work to paint, or repaint. Lots of nooks and crannies, corners and crevices.

But that teal just called to me. It wasn't aqua or cyan, but the perfect love child. Could I pull it off? Would I be happy with something other than my status quo?

Throwing caution to the wind, I grabbed a paint chip. "Kiss and Teal." I read softly, rubbing my finger across the surface. Was I being reckless? Was this a mistake? Was I being impulsive?

"It's just paint," I said, again aloud, even though I was talking to myself. "If I don't like it, I'm not stuck with it. I can always change my mind."

A guy wearing white painter's clothes standing a few feet away gave me a sideways glance.

Commending myself for making a decision, trying

something new, and giving myself permission to change my mind, I went to where the paint base was stacked in the next aisle over and chose one that would work.

While waiting at the counter to get my paint mixed, my thoughts wandered to Grant.

Did he need anything? I could text him, or call him. I did have his number.

No, I shouldn't. That might seem too much of a busybody.

But, if he did need something, I was already here and it would save him a trip.

He's going to think I'm weird.

Or just being neighborly.

You're way overthinking this.

I am.

Oh, just call him. It can't hurt.

Before I could change my mind or talk myself out of it, I surrendered to my inner voice. I pulled out my phone and called him.

"Hey," he said when he picked up the phone.

"I'm at Home Depot, do you need anything?"

"That's weird. I'm at Home Depot too."

I immediately looked around to see if he was standing behind me somehow, watching me call him. "Where?"

"Plumbing. Where are you?"

"Paint. I'm almost done. Want me to come find you?"

"I'll meet you there. I need some spray paint."

The paint associate daubed the perfectly pretty teal on the lid before using a mallet to secure the lid. He slid it across the counter to me and I fell in love all over again. This was a good choice. Gripping the thin, metal handle, I carried the weighted pail over to the spray paint cage to meet Grant. While waiting, I checked out what was new in the world of spray paint.

Beside the rolling cage door, was a display of brooms. What an odd place to put brooms. Was there something fancy-dancy about them that was new and innovative? I wished most household cleaning tools could be as versatile as my fluffy duster. The extension feature was hands-down my favorite thing.

I pulled a broom out and tapped it on the floor. Nothing about the broom seemed better than the one I currently had. Maybe it wasn't anything special, but placed here to encourage impulse purchases.

"Oh, look," a mocking voice said. It came from the kid wearing the baseball hat, fluorescent green t-shirt that read "Waterberry Construction", jeans and dirty, yellow work boots. He stood in front of the spray paint display. "It's the witch. Are ya shopping for a new broom?"

As I turned to face him, my grip tightened around the broom stick. His dirty blond hair was a little longer, and his frame not so skinny, but I still knew who he was, and he was no longer a kid. He had to be in his early twenties by now. "Oh, look, it's Dirk the Delinquent," I said. Hopefully he'd grown-up since the last time I saw him. "Off to deface someone else's property?"

He scowled at me. "Whatever, Witch."

Nope, no new maturity detected.

"Does your parole officer know you're here?" Whether or not he had any more run-ins with the law since the last time I saw him, when he egged my house, I didn't know. But I thought it was safe to assume in this case.

He snorted. "No."

No, he didn't have one, or no, the parole officer didn't know he was here? "Are you legally old enough to buy spray paint?"

"Why do you care?"

"Because you'd be charged as an adult if you get caught," I said. Which he'd deserve. Just saying.

He rolled his eyes at me. "Whatever, Witch," he said again before stalking away.

"Is that all you've got?" I called after him, shaking the broom in the air. He disappeared around the corner. I debated chasing after him, making a last-ditch effort to swat him with those stiff bristles. But I wasn't really looking to get arrested for assault today. And last time I "interacted" with him, it didn't go so well for me.

"Kate?"

Grant stood behind me.

"What was that all about?" he asked.

I inhaled deeply and carefully placed the broom back in the display. "He's one of the high school kids who started the rumor that I was a witch three years ago. Like a real witch, not just the kind you dress up as for Halloween." I exhaled, letting the after-effects of the confrontation go. "I called the cops on them because they were vandalizing Haunty—sorry, your house—one night. When I yelled at them, they ran away. But I called the police, and they got picked up by the police. That kid's dad happened was on the town council, so he got them off. On Halloween night, they came and egged my house. I chased them down, waving a broom, throwing my own eggs at them, screaming and yelling. I tackled one, that one, but he got away. When I called the cops, they said the kids claimed they saw me doing weird things. Like black magic things."

"Were you?"

I scoffed. "No, of course not. The strongest stuff I was using back then was Mod Podge. They made it all up. But, of course, people became curious. You know how gossip is."

"Gossip is never up to any good."

"Exactly. But they were seniors in high school, so I'm sure it made its way around school and spread from there. So that's how I got the reputation of being a witch." Avoiding people on purpose didn't help my cause.

"So that's the history of Kate."

"Some of it," I said. There was so much more, but that was enough true confessions for one day. "What about the history of Grant?" Weren't we doing this whole *I-share-something-you-share-something* thing?

"That's a long story. But right now, I'm hungry. Have you eaten?" he asked. "'Cause I haven't eaten. Want to grab a sandwich or something?"

17

KATE

I stared at Grant standing against the spray paint cage.

Did I?

I didn't know.

I kind of did. I *was* hungry.

But I kind of didn't.

Having my paint in hand made me want to rush home and start my project.

But...food. And I found Grant less annoying these days. Really, there was no need to rush. I could take an hour out of my day and get lunch with him. "How do you feel about lobster?" I asked.

He nodded. "I like lobster."

"Good. Seafood can be a polarizing food topic."

"I like seafood, but not a fan of oysters on the half shell."

I curled my lips and scrunched my nose. "Yuck. Me, neither! It's like sucking snot."

His brows went up. "That's one way to describe it."

"I was thinking lobster rolls. You know, seafood and sandwich all rolled up into one."

He laughed and bumped my shoulder. "I see what you did there. Lobster roll. Rolled up in one. Ha, ha."

"That's me, funny as ever," I said.

"Lobster rolls sound great."

We checked out and decided to take his car to the restaurant. I put my paint in the trunk, locked my car and climbed into his passenger seat. I directed him through town, pointing out the local places of interest if we passed any.

"That's Fremmer's Bakery. They have the best chocolate mousse pie," I said. A few miles later I pointed to the next "landmark." From above the tree line, you could see the red, winding rollercoaster tracks. "There's Gainesville Amusement Park, where my sister works."

Grant ducked his neck to get a better look through the windshield as we drove by. "It doesn't stay open year-round, I assume."

"Nope. Opens Memorial Day and closes Labor Day. Then only weekends until Halloween."

"So, it closes next weekend?" he asked.

"Yes, but it also hosts special events like concerts, holiday parties and private parties. My wedding on Halloween was scheduled there." I don't know why I volunteered that. I didn't mean to.

"That's a weird day to have a wedding." His mouth opened and he gave me a funny look. "What's the draw? You can dress up in costumes for the wedding?"

I shrugged as images of my wedding ceremony site came to mind. *Halloween with a Splash of Fall.* It would've been perfect. Photoshoot-perfect. I was so proud of what I had put together. "I loved Halloween. The fall. The pumpkins, the leaves, the cool air, pumpkin spice."

"It didn't sound that way to me when I caught you bad-talking those pumpkins at the store," he said.

"You're right about that."

"If you could do it all over again, would you?"

"Get married on Halloween?" I assumed that's what he meant. "Nope. That ship has wrecked."

Grant glanced at me. "Meaning your wedding?"

"Meaning my almost-wedding. And yes, that's the reason." It didn't take a genius to figure that out.

"Makes sense," he said quietly.

"At that next street, take a right," I said, pointing out where the waterfront restaurant was. I was ready for a change in conversation. Sean had been on my mind far too much lately.

"This is a restaurant?" he asked, taking in the large white tent that covered most of the area and the picnic tables set up two by two with a path down the middle. The "restaurant" was really two trailers positioned adjacent to each other.

Grant frowned as he surveyed the property doubtfully, his head slowly turning from one side of the lot to the other.

"I know it looks like a tourist trap, but it's actually really good," I said in way of explanation.

"I'm going to have to trust you on this," he said. "You're the local."

We climbed out of the car and approached the first trailer. A menu board written in bright markers advertised the day's specials.

"I'm gonna stick with my original plan and get a lobster roll," I said.

Grant squinted at the board attached to the side of the trailer. "Looks like there's lots of good stuff, but I'm with you on this one. Lobster roll it is."

We ordered our meals, paid and went to the next trailer's window and were handed a paper plate with our food: an over-sized hot dog bun with chunks of pink and white meat coated in mayonnaise. Yum! I could already taste its deliciousness.

We chose one of the grey, picnic tables and sat opposite one another.

"Are you sure I'm going to like this?" He picked up the roll and examined it closely, then sniffed it.

"Would I ever steer you wrong?" I asked.

Our eyes met. "Um, I think I recall a certain someone telling me to call 1-800-SHUT-OFF-WATER when I had my water leak."

My cheeks burned. "That was before I liked you."

His eyes held mine and he leaned in. "So, you like me now?"

The heat in my face grew. It was probably up to my eyebrows by now. "You know, knew you."

He considered the sandwich.

"I promise, it's good."

I watched as he took a bite, seeing his expression go from cautious to relaxed as he chewed. "You're right, this is good." Chunks of meat fell out of his roll as he took another bite.

"I told you," I said, then helped myself to my sandwich.

We are in hungry silence.

After the last bite, he wiped his mouth with a napkin, leaned back in his chair and patted his stomach. "That was good," he said.

"Ready for dessert?" I asked.

He squinted back at the trailer with the menu board on the sign. "They have dessert here?"

"Not here." I shook my head. "But my friend has an apple stand not far from here."

His eyebrows came together in confusion. "An apple? To me, that's breakfast."

Once in the car, I explained more. "They're caramel apples, but she has all different flavors. It really is a dessert."

He started the engine, turned on the air, and I directed him to Becky's place, which was really her family's house and moped business. "Appley Ever After" was a little shed and a few picnic tables with umbrellas in front of it.

Becky's face lit up as we approached. She walked outside to greet us. Her blond hair was pulled up in a high ponytail and her blue eyes sparkled almost as much as her huge diamond engagement ring. "Hey, Kate. How are you?" She hugged me.

"Good," I said. I laid my hand on Grant's forearm. I noticed how soft his skin was, but just for a quick second. "This is my neighbor, Grant, the one who bought the house."

"My mom's associate brokered the sale," Becky said. She reached out and shook his hand. "You're a brave man."

"Stupid would be more appropriate," Grant said honestly.

I waved away his comment. "More like naïve."

"Naïve?" Becky asked, looking from me to him. "You didn't know what the house looked like before you bought it? I thought it was posted online."

"It was," he said. "But I had no idea how much work it would be."

"Good thing Kate's your neighbor. She's like little Miss Fixer-Up."

I glanced at Grant. He looked over at me and our eyes met. "I'm finding that out." He held my look for a moment longer than I could and I ended up looking away. "She's an expert when it comes to popcorn ceilings," he added.

"So, you've been working on ceilings, huh?" Becky said, with one eyebrow raised suggestively.

"Not today," I said. The silence was a moment too long. "We ran into each other at Home Depot and decided to grab lunch and now dessert," I said

"You came to the right place," Becky said, wiping her hands on her apple-green apron. Her engagement ring flashed in the sunlight. "What can I get you?"

Her display case was simple, with six trays of apples. There was plain caramel, white chocolate caramel, cookies 'n' cream, chocolate caramel, salted caramel, and pumpkin spice.

"Little early for the Halloween flavor, don't you think?" I was definitely not going for the despised pumpkin spice.

"It's one of my most popular flavors. When September first hits, I bust it out."

At least it wasn't July fifth.

"I'm still going to stick with my favorite white chocolate caramel," I said.

Grant studied the case. "I have no idea. They all look so good. I'll try the salted caramel."

"They are all good," Becky said, smiling.

We tried to pay, but Becky insisted they were on the house.

"How's the engagement going? Have a date decided yet?" Last time I spoke to her, spring of the following year had been decided, but no date had been nailed down.

Becky looked at her ring and then back at me, her face glowing. "May. The weekend before the park officially opens."

"They're getting married at the Gainesville Amusement Park," I told Grant.

"Weddings? There? Seriously?" Grant asked. "Don't you guys have churches in this town?"

"Her fiancé's family owns the park," I said.

"Oh, okay," Grant said.

Becky let out a small laugh. "They try to do everything there that will bring in revenue. It's still just getting back on its feet financially."

"I see," Grant said. He glanced at his watch and Becky had more customers arrive, so we said goodbye and headed back to Home Depot.

Our silent drive home was interrupted by my phone dinging.

Becky: Were you on a DATE?

A GIF of big wide eyes popped up next.

While Grant turned left at an intersection, I quickly typed a response.

Me: No. Spontaneous outing.

My phone dinged. I didn't look at it, not wanting Grant to think I was distracted. I took a quick second to peak at my screen while he navigated the car.

Becky: You could count that as a date.
Me: I don't.

"Sorry," I apologized. "That's Becky."

"Comparing notes?" Grant asked, grinning at me.

"Something like that, I guess. Asking if we were on a date."

"Were we?" His voice was soft.

I didn't know how to answer it, so I answered it as honestly as I could. "I don't know."

The conversation went silent.

"Let me know when you decide what this was," he finally said.

"Okay?" Still awkward.

Thankfully, Grant pulled into the Home Depot parking lot soon after, so we didn't have to analyze any more semantics or have it lead into exploring our feelings. He parked in the spot beside my car. "Here you are."

"Thank you," I said.

"Text me when you're available for the popcorn party."

I opened the car door and got one leg out. "Okay. But it won't be today. I'm a little peopled out," I said.

"I'll beat you home," Grant said playfully and shooed me out of the car.

He probably would, since Becky texted me again, and I took the time to read it.

Becky: Sometimes you're no fun.

Me: Sometimes, but not today. I was a lotta fun.

I included a winky emoji at the end before hitting send.

I climbed in my car, with a smile on my face, and placed my phone face down so I wouldn't be tempted to text and drive.

SEPTEMBER

18

KATE

My wedding assignment at work hung over me like a dark thunder cloud. And thinking about someone else's wedding just dredged up memories of my own almost-wedding. Thoughts of my failed relationship with Sean haunted me during my workday. I was over it and didn't need to rehash it. Anymore. But thinking of his current relationship irked me. Which was why I tried to never think about it. It put me in a bad mood.

I tried to compartmentalize my thoughts about him into the back of my brain and concentrate on work, but stocking shelves didn't require much thought today. I was restocking scrapbook paper, so as long as the printed side was up, I was good. The memories kept coming.

It was easy to see people for who they were when watching a dating show like *Desperately Seeking Mr. Right*, but had I seen Sean's true colors when I dated him? Chrissy never liked him and she was usually spot on.

I thought back to our interactions when we first met. He moved here out of school to take his first job on the local news. His parents lived in town, so he stayed with them while getting established.

Our biggest, most glaring difference was his ambition versus mine. He wanted to move to a big city and work for a bigger news channel and I was perfectly comfortable in my life. I loved where I lived, loved what I was doing and had my family close by. I wasn't looking to change any of that. That was the first crack in our relationship.

I slipped the next pile of paper into the slot and felt the sting of a paper cut.

"Katherine, you're needed in the back office. Katherine to the back office." Robyn's voice blasted over the walkie-talkie. I turned the volume dial way down, sighed, and abandoned my stack of paper. I needed a Band Aid anyway.

I weighed the reasons I'd be summoned. I was either in trouble, or it had to do with the celebrity wedding. Honestly, it could be either. The meeting with the Kelly had been rescheduled twice now, while the bride collected "inspo."

I pressed on my finger as I walked to the office.

It wasn't Robyn in her office.

I saw the platinum blond hair before I heard his voice. "Miss Katherine!" Kelly smiled as I approached.

What was he doing here? I was almost one-hundred-percent certain there was nothing scheduled for today.

"Kelly," I said in my most pleasant customer service saccharine voice. "How may I help you?" The worst part about the assignment wasn't helping, so much as it was pretending to be happy to help. Actually, Kelly was cool. If only we were working on *anything* other than a wedding together.

But I ~~wanted~~ needed to keep my job, so I would suck it up and dig deep to find the former, nicer version of Kate.

He lifted a white foam poster board and leaned it the seat of a chair. "I wanted to drop this by."

"What is it?" I asked.

With the flick of a wrist, he spun it around. "Tada! A vision board!" He propped the board up on a chair and completed the action with jazz hands.

My bottom lip slowly dropped open as I took a step closer. My eyes traveled from one picture to the next to the next.

"It's amazing, I *know*. My client is very decisive about what she wants and very detail-oriented."

I stared at it, gobsmacked. I couldn't believe what I was seeing. It *was* amazing.

"Fabulous, don't you think," he said.

I looked him straight on. "What I think is those pictures are subject to copyright."

Kelly's hand went to his chest. "Yes, my client got these off of Pinterest, but..."

I pointed to the board. "Pinterest doesn't give people the right to rip off *someone's* photos, never mind her *whole* wedding," I yelled.

Kelly, still with his hand to his chest, took a step back.

"Who is your client?" I asked, eerily calm. The drumming of my pulse picked up intensity.

"I'm sorry. I can't share that information."

I wished I had my broom so I could beat it out of him. Just kidding. But the thought did cross my mind.

I snatched the posterboard from where Kelly had propped it up. "This," I jabbed at the first picture, then the next, then another random one. "These are from my wedding, in the exact order I had them."

Kelly's eyes became saucers.

If I got fired for this little outburst, oh, well. "I'm going to ask you again. Who. Is. Your. Client?"

This board was evidence of full-on stalking. I had a stalker. Ripping off my wedding. Next thing you'd know, she'd want to talk over my life. Who was this crazy lady?

"Merry Webber."

"Oh!" was all I managed. Merry Webber! I should've known! The Mistress of Christmas. My YouTube nemesis. My ex-fiancé's fiancée. I grumbled and growled. "Why, that no-good-man-stealing-wedding-copying-counterfeiter! She's—"

Kelly broke in. "I'm sorry, but I don't understand how we went from vision board to meltdown."

I picked up the vision board and snapped it over my knee. "The Queen of Halloween does *not* plan weddings for The Mistress of Christmas."

I dropped the bent board and it landed on the dirty, beige linoleum with a tap, bottom side down so it looked like an odd tent from an elementary school student project.

"Wait. That's you? You're Kate Renovates?" Kelly asked, shocked.

"Sure am, baby," I said

"Oh, my gosh! I thought you looked familiar! I *loved* you. Where've you been hiding, girl?"

"Living the dream here at Hawley's Hobbies," I said over my shoulder before I marched off.

I felt glorious and majestic as I strode through the store. Triumphant music played in my head as I peeled my apron off and flung it carelessly to the side, seeing it land on a metal flamingo. I pulled my hair from the ponytail that squeezed my brain and let it fall loose over my shoulders.

It was a scene straight out of a girl boss empowerment

movie and I applauded myself as I walked to the employee lunch room and gathered my stuff. With the flick of my foot, I kicked my locker shut and slung my bag over my shoulder. Keys jingling in my hand, I headed to the main exit of the store.

"Katherine!" Robyn barked.

I froze, three feet from the exit. Customers at the checkout counters paused what they were doing and for a moment, time stood still.

Oh, crap! I hadn't really thought this through.

I turned, slowly, not sure what wrath I would face.

Robyn strode over. "In my office, please," she said, her voice controlled. "Now." Her eyebrows going practically into her hairline reinforced her command.

I spun on my heel and marched theatrically behind Robyn. At this point, I had nothing to lose.

Kelly was no longer in Robyn's office, thank goodness. Robyn shut the door with force, which would keep my censure private. Robyn's arm shot out straight, pointing to her wall. "What was that?" she said.

"That was me resigning from my special assignment."

"You did more than resign with that stunt, Kate. You got yourself fired."

∽

So, I got fired.

I hoofed it to my car.

Big whoop.

And climbed in and slammed the door shut.

At least I left with my dignity in tact and could probably get unemployment.

I hoped.

I'd never been fired before or applied for unemployment.

Whatever. I'll figure it out.

Anything is better than contributing to Merry Webber's wedding.

I spun out of the parking lot and jumped into traffic. Horns blared.

Which was basically my wedding.

And no one gets to have my wedding but me!

Another horn sounded as merged in front of a car in the right lane.

I swear, all that girl did was rip everything off from me. My ideas. My wedding. My fiancé. *Get your own life, Merry Webber!*

I drove like Cruella de Ville as I sped home. I maintained my reckless streak by calling Chrissy.

"What's up?" Chrissy said.

"I just got fired," I said, gripping the phone to my ear.

"You WHAT?"

"Got fired."

"HOLY CRAP!" Chrissy yelled. "They *fired* you?"

"I know! Well, I tried to quit, but then Robyn fired me," I said, recounting the story.

"Why?"

"Because you'd never guess who the famous person is?"

"The famous person?"

I probably needed to clue Chrissy in on what was going on. "You know, for the celebrity wedding? Kelly, the wedding planner came in today and I found out Merry Webber is his client."

"But she's not famous! She's a hack!" Chrissy exclaimed.

"EXACTLY!"

"What are you going to do?" Chrissy asked.

"I don't know," I said and hung up.

Everything I thought of was probably not a good idea.

∽

I was wound up and ready to work. At home. On my projects. Not *her* wedding. I dragged the headboard from the garage to the She Shed.

How dare she steal my wedding!

I grabbed a drop cloth, shook it out with a snap of the fabric and spread it on the floor.

She already stole my man!

I shook the paint can violently.

I swear, that girl doesn't have one original bone in her body.

I'd like to break every bone in her body.

I grabbed a screwdriver and popped the lid off. Air bubbles floated to the top.

Okay, maybe not. I just didn't like her.

I really, really, really *didn't like her.*

I mixed up the chalk powder and stirred it into the beautiful teal paint. Oh, it was lovely.

I took a breath. I just needed to focus on the furniture right now and forget about *her* and *him* and *work*.

Out of habit I got my phone stand out and started filming it. Not to post on YouTube, but just for me to document my progress.

With a dip of the brush and a swipe of the paint, the transformation started. Gone were the signs of wear and tear, the little imperfections and the faded sunspots. Instead, was a vibrant happy hue.

And who cares if she stole Sean. He obviously was complicit with being stolen.

They deserve each other.

As I aggressively slapped on the paint, thoughts bubbled to the surface. As they came, I mentally painted over them.

You got my man, fine, keep him.

I spread the paint up, then down. I pictured painting over her face. She now looked like one of those guys in the Blue Man Group, but with flaming red hair.

But I am NOT planning your wedding.

And I am NOT rolling over so you can replace me in my creative kingdom.

"I am not going down without a fight!" I declared triumphantly as I stepped back to take in my work. I had missed this.

"Meow."

I spun around, paintbrush in hand, and found Midnight sitting in the threshold, watching me.

"Hey, Middy. How'd you get out? Come to watch me paint? Support me in my—"

Grant appeared in the doorway. "Knock knock."

He pointed to the headboard with a stack of paint chip samples. "Looking good."

"Thank you," I said. I pointed to the cat. "Look who decided to show up."

"Yeah, I saw her over here and thought I'd check out what you ladies are up to."

Without waiting for an invitation, he walked past me and sat down on the purple velvet Victorian sofa.

I didn't protest his inviting himself in. Obviously, it was futile.

"I thought you were coming over to cut my lawn," I joked.

"I could do that later today."

"Great," I said. I hoped that would be the end of the

conversation and that he'd go home. Midnight was okay to stay.

He gave the sofa a bounce test. "This isn't comfortable at all," he said. "And it doesn't seem your style."

It wasn't, but I didn't like guests when I worked, either. "It was free. And purple. I'm usually working, so I don't sit on it very much." Especially since I hadn't been in the shed for the last few years. The sofa itself had great lines and great legs, but the cushion was thin and slightly flat.

He pointed to my work area. "Are you having a paint party?"

"Yeah. I needed to get the furniture out of the garage."

"Were they causing trouble? I heard you telling Midnight about a fight."

Exactly how much had he heard?

I cleared my throat. "More like I caused the trouble."

His eyebrows rose. "Being a troublemaker, are you?"

"I got fired today," I said. It sounded strange to hear myself say it. It was still fresh and raw and adrenaline rushed through me. I gripped the paintbrush as the angry feelings returned.

"Oh," Grant said quietly. "That's not good."

"No, it's not. But I'll figure something out. But for now, I'm going to paint furniture. Painting makes me feel better."

"How about I mow your lawn now? Having short grass will make you feel better. Unless you want me to hang out and you can tell me more about your bad day."

The way he held my gaze made my stomach twist in a weird way. It made me want to take a mental snapshot of that moment and keep it tucked away.

Then I realized with happiness and a side of horror, that he made my stomach go mushy.

I was in trouble. In more ways than one.

19

GRANT

Tuesday
Me: Hey. You, me and the last of the popcorn ceilings tonight? You up for it?
Kate: Can't. Busy.
Me: Ok
Wednesday
Me: How's today or tonight for scraping?
Kate: Still busy.
Me: With what?
Kate: Painting.
Thursday
Me: Got plans for Friday night?
Kate: Not really.
Me: Time to tackle the ceilings?
Kate:
Friday
Me: Are you avoiding me?
Kate: ??
Me: I haven't seen you all week.
Kate: It's been busy.

She was definitely avoiding me, although I couldn't figure out why. I came up with a plan that was sure to get some answers. That plan: Operation Ice Cream.

She opened the door, which I was kind of surprised about. But then again, the lights were on and I could hear the TV, so it'd be hard to pretend she wasn't home.

"Are you avoiding me?" I asked immediately. "Just for my own ego, is it me or the popcorn ceilings?"

Surprise flickered across her face. "I'm still painting the bedroom set. And, some job-hunting."

I held up the box. "I brought ice cream bars. You can say no to me, but you can't say no to Ben and Jerry."

There was a hint of a smile. "The true language of love."

"If you let me in, I'll share them with you."

She stepped aside without a word.

I walked to the kitchen and set the box on the table.

"Want one now?" I asked.

"Of course," she said.

She sat down across from me. I handed her a chocolate fudge brownie bar.

"How much more do you have to paint?"

She bit into the bar; the shell cracked under pressure. "It's just about done. I need to do the second coat on the nightstand and then wax it and then I'm done."

I was impressed. "Really? Can I see it?"

"You can do one better. You can help me carry it in."

"I walked right in to that one," I joked.

She nibbled at the edge of her the bar. "Yeah, pretty much."

I held up the bar. "I'd be happy to help once I finish my ice cream."

She smiled. "I hoped you'd say that."

She wasn't kidding when she said the furniture was

finished. It was a blue green color. On the dresser and vanity, she'd painted the outside frame and left the drawers the original brown, wood finish. The bed frame was completely painted. I thought it looked good, considering how worn out and faded it had looked when I gave it to her. The nightstand was on a work table, drawers out with the primer coat on.

"Nice job," I said. "Now where is this going inside?"

"Upstairs. Bedroom sets usually go in the bedroom."

Having never seen her upstairs and knowing she had lived here for at least a few years, I assumed all her rooms were furnished. "Do we need to take stuff out first?"

"Nope," she said.

I inwardly groaned at the thought of carrying all that furniture up a flight of stairs, but I could suck it up.

We carried the headboard and then the footboard. We leaned them against the wall in the hall outside the bedroom.

She stood in front of the closed door, her hand on the knob. "Now, once I show you these rooms, you're in my circle of trust," said Kate.

What's the big secret? "That's a good thing, right? I mean, unless that circle is a pentagram or something."

"You're funny. I thought we'd already established I wasn't a witch."

"If I really thought you were a witch, I wouldn't step foot in your house."

"I don't go showing the spare bedrooms to just anyone."

How many people came to visit her? Really? Bill made it seem like I was taking my life in my own hands even talking to her, but every single "myth" about her had been dispelled. The more time I spent with her, the more I liked her.

"Okay. I'm honored to be in your circle of trust."

She opened the bedroom door and the room was nothing like downstairs. It was like an alternate universe. The room was dark and the curtains pulled shut. There was enough light peeking through to see that orange bins lined three of the four walls. Black feather boas, lace and white mesh ghosts were just some of the things I could identify that were piled high on top of the bins.

I set the headboard against the only available wall and looked around the room, taking it all in. I never suspected she had this much Halloween stuff. "When I met you, you were talking smack to the pumpkins. I thought you didn't like Halloween."

"I never said that."

I had so many questions. "You *do* like Halloween?"

"Not as much as I used to."

And something poking out and curling up...was that a squid? Or an octopus tentacle?

"What is that?" I pointed to the unidentified underwater sea creature part.

"The cobweb or the tentacle?"

"The tentacle." I took a step closer. "Can I touch it?" I asked.

She shrugged. "If you want."

I took a closer look. It was round and rubber and looked about eight feet long. "Why do you have this?"

"I made it."

"For what?" Why would anyone need a tentacle?

"For Halloween. I have a ship—"

I cut in. "A ship? Like a pirate ship? Why?"

"It was part of a yard display."

"Did you make that?"

She nodded. "I did. With pallets. It was part of a yard display."

I pointed to the stacks of bins. "And all this stuff?"

"More decorations."

"All this is for yard decorations?" It was a lot. At least twenty-five bins. Probably more.

"Yes. Shall we get the rest of the furniture?"

I backed out of the room, still curious about the contents of the bins. I had never met someone that had so many decorations. Especially Halloween. I could understand, possibly, Christmas, but Halloween? I still hadn't made it to that part of her YouTube videos yet.

"Why do, or did, you like Halloween so much?"

She shrugged a shoulder. "It's the holiday of imagination. You can be anything, explore your creativity, make-believe. It was a great creative outlet."

"Okay," I said, and didn't press more.

The dresser was easy to handle and went into the room with the bed. The dressing table was a little harder because the size of the mirror made it hard to balance. We set that down in the hall by the other bedroom door.

"We're going to put that in here," she said and jerked her thumb at the door.

I wondered what decorative surprises waited behind door number two. Christmas was my guess. One room for Halloween, one for Christmas. I wondered if there was Valentine's and Easter stuff in her basement. Her downstairs was neat and tidy, with no ounce of decoration for any holiday that would serve as a clue to this stash of stuff.

She opened the door, and light didn't flood out of this one either. It was just as dark as the other ones, curtains closed. And more orange bins. "More Halloween?" I asked.

"Remember I said if I showed you these rooms, you were in my circle of trust."

I nodded.

"That means no judgment on my stuff."

"I had no idea you had this much Halloween stuff."

"This was actually my wedding decorations."

I closed my mouth so I wouldn't say something stupid. Given the dim lighting, it was hard to make out everything exactly, but it looked similar to the contents of the bins in the other room. Minus the tentacle.

"Let's go see if we can wrangle that wardrobe up here. We might need to wait for when Bill comes tomorrow to ask for his help."

She looked around the room, her shoulders drooped as if the ghosts of the past weighed on her. "I think that's enough for today. I don't think there's enough room in here and it's too heavy to carry up the stairs."

I stepped back to get a better look at the space and see if we could move things around to make the space, but bumped into one of the smaller stacked bins beside the door. It crashed to the floor, the plastic lid popped off and dozens and dozens of black spiders escaped.

"Oops," I said. I knew they weren't real, but leaned down to take a closer look. "Sorry."

She picked up the lid, which now had a jagged piece broken off the corner and set it aside. "It's a hazard of having so much stuff."

I got to my knees and grabbed the bin. "Sorry about your container. I'll replace it," I said. I grabbed a handful of spiders, then stopped. "These are weird," I said, giving them a squeeze. They were squishy.

She joined me on the floor and plucked one from my

hand. Her skin brushing mine was distracting. It took me a second to recover.

She tossed it back in the bin. "They're silicone. Awesome, right?"

Silicone spiders had actually never crossed my mind. "I guess in the right situation they could be pretty cool. Like, say, getting revenge on someone you hate. Or pulling a prank on someone who hates spiders."

"I have silicone bats too," she said, sounding delighted.

Bats made me think of opening my garage door. "Why use fake ones when I have real ones in my garage?"

We both reached for some spiders at the same time and our hands touched. Another spark went through me.

"I'll keep that in mind if I ever need a colony of live bats," she said, her cheeks turning red.

"I'll even give them to you. Just to be neighborly."

20

KATE

*O*ur hands touched and a little current passed between us. I pulled back my hand from the shock. Not the surprise, but the touch.

It was static from the carpet. Obviously.

I frantically grabbed at more spiders. If I kept busy, the weirdness would pass and the situation would go back to normal.

But it didn't. I looked up, expecting to see Grant searching for scattered spiders. Instead, our eyes met.

Time seemed to slow down. He reached out and took a lock of my hair and curled it around his finger. I felt the electricity again. "I like you, Kate," he said, his voice soft.

My heart sped up into panic mode.

What is going on?

What am I doing?!

I wanted to snatch my hair from him and scoot back to put some space in between us. But I didn't.

"Did you put a spell on me?" he asked slowly, holding my gaze.

Did I put a spell on him?

Was he crazy?

I was the one acting like I had the spell on me. Being all mushy and teenage-girly being gaga over my crush. I gulped. "No," was all I managed.

My heart pounded so hard I could feel it in my ears.

He leaned in.

I realized I leaned in.

What am I—

His lips touched mine and I lost all train of thought. I closed my eyes and breathed in, ignoring the spiderweb of thoughts spreading in my head. His lips were soft, inviting, warm. Gravity pulled me closer to him and I went with it.

The kiss ended slower than it began.

After a few lingering kisses, we broke apart.

"I've been wanting to do that for a while now," he said.

He had?

That was unexpected.

Him kissing me was even more unexpected.

Me kissing him back? I did *not* see that coming.

∼

When Grant left, I shut the door behind him and leaned on it to steady myself. I groaned quietly. What just happened? I made out with Grant in the Halloween room, that's what happened.

Chrissy's face filled my phone screen as her ring tone broke the silence. I jumped. Did she have a sixth sense or something?

I took a deep breath and tried to sound calm. "Hey, what's going on?"

"Did you hear about the power outage at the park? All the computers went down for a couple of hours."

"No, I didn't." Why? Because I was too busy making out with my neighbor.

"It was crazy..." Chrissy went on.

Did I have kisser's remorse? No, not really. The kiss had been amazing. *Really* amazing. And I liked Grant. Not *like*-liked him, or at least I didn't think of him that way B.K. (Before Kiss). Kissing him hadn't been anywhere on my radar. So where did we go from here? Did I *want* to go *there* with him? What if things didn't work out?

"Are you listening?" Chrissy asked.

Her words shook me from my thoughts. "What? Yeah, I'm here."

"You seem distracted."

Yeah, you could say that.

"What'd I just tell you?" she asked.

I don't know.

I took a deep breath. I couldn't believe I was about to admit this. "I kissed him," I blurted out to Chrissy.

"Him who?" She asked. "What are you talking about?"

Him *who*? Did she even have to *ask*? Were there any other men in my life? "Grant."

I could hear an intake of breath. "I knew it! I *knew* there was something going on with you two!"

Damage-control instinct kicked in and I tried to downplay it. "Not really. He comes over a lot, but not enough to qualify as 'something going on'."

"Uh-huh."

"Usually, it's to take a break. Today he helped me move furniture," I said.

"That sounds all very contrived," Chrissy said, sounding amused.

I made my way to the couch and sat on the edge of it. "I don't know." I really didn't.

"And?" Chrissy said.

"I spilled some spiders and we both bent down to pick up them up and..."

"Are you sure it was an accident? That sounds like a ploy."

"And that's when we kissed," I said.

"And?"

What did she want from me? "And what?"

"There has to be more to it. Did your eyes meet?"

I rolled my eyes, even though she couldn't see me. "This isn't a romance novel."

"Technically, it kinda is. It's the start of a new story and I want to know what happened. It's been a very long time, so let's hear all the details. It's a good thing, Martha Stewart!"

"It's *not* a good thing. If we break up then I have to live next to him for however long he lives there, which might be a very long time."

She *tsk*ed me. "Why are you already dooming the relationship when it hasn't even started? Give love a chance."

I flopped into a reclining position and propped my feet on the arm rest. "It was really more a kiss opportunity than of feelings. He's lonely, I'm lonely, our faces were inches apart and it seemed like the thing to do."

Chrissy laughed out loud. "You actually admitted you're lonely. Wow, Kate, making progress in your path to self-discovery."

"Ha ha," I deadpanned.

"You've been lonely for a long time and haven't made out with other lonely men. There are plenty of them around if you go looking. So, if you needed the opportunity, it was readily available. And if you're looking for motive—"

"Chrissy," I interrupted, "this isn't a mystery you need to solve. We kissed. End of story."

I heard a low chuckle.

"More like beginning of story," she said.

I was about to object, both to her and the crazy thoughts running around in my head, when Chrissy continued. "Just go with it. You might be surprised where it takes you. Don't you deserve a second chance at happiness?"

I was torn.

Did I want to go with it?

Maybe I *did* deserve a second chance at happiness.

I knew what I *didn't* want.

I didn't want to turn into a giddy pile of goo.

But here I was, being gooey.

But I couldn't help it.

I'd forgotten how kissing felt. The warmth of his lips, his breath on my skin. The smell of his aftershave. No wonder why people read romance novels, it created this rush of dopamine and I was not exempt. I was *swimming* in dopamine.

21

KATE

I had to sell the bedroom set. I didn't want to, but I had bills to pay. The online marketplace site was opened on my laptop, but I was still not ready to list my beloved furniture. Instead, I sat on my couch staring daggers at the screen.

A light tap on the door sounded before it opened a little. Grant poked his head in. "You home?" His hair was messy in a cute, boyish way and he had smudge of paint on his forehead. He must've been painting this week.

I fell back into the couch and sighed. "Come on in."

"You seem thrilled to see me," he said.

I pointed at the computer. "It's not you, it's this."

There had been lots of "adult" conversations I'd had with myself since the kiss and I came to the conclusion that it'd be okay to dip my toe in the dating pool again. But just my toe. You know, to take it slow.

He sat beside me and glanced at the computer screen. "You buying furniture?"

I frowned. "I wish. I have to sell the set you gave me."

"But you love that set!" he said. "You can't sell it."

True. I did. "But I love eating even more. And I haven't found a job yet."

Grant was quiet for a few moments before sitting up and angling his body toward me. "Would you consider working for me?"

My face scrunched in confusion. "You came over to offer me a job?"

"No, but I have more work than I can do myself, and you're way more capable than me of doing it, so work with me until you find something better."

Tempting. No customer service. No uniform. No set hours. Very tempting. "Will you pay me with real money or pizza and ice cream? Because as much as I like pizza and ice cream, I can't pay the bills with that."

He chuckled. "Real money, of course. Pizza and ice cream would be a fringe benefit." After a beat he added, "And me as your co-worker."

It didn't take a genius to see the benefits to *that* offer. "Okay, I'll do it."

He brightened. "Really?"

A small sense of relief settled over me. "Yes," I said. I scooched over closer to him. He took my hand.

"Okay, so now for the real reason I'm here."

I lifted my eyebrow. "There's more?"

"I have a proposal for you," he said.

I sat up straight. "We've only been kissing, don't rush things," I said, and winked.

"It's not that kind of a proposal, but it is kind of a big ask."

What could it be? His last big ask was popcorn ceilings, which was more of a big chore. If I had to do it all again, I would've suggested using beadboard to cover it all up.

"I want to decorate my yard for Halloween and I want

you to help."

Questions floated through my head and I needed clarification. "Meaning?"

"As we know, other than live bats, I have nothing and the former owners didn't leave anything spooky in the garage. And you practically have a warehouse upstairs. Could I borrow some or your decorations and would you help me set up my yard?"

"Only your yard?"

"My house is scary enough without decorations."

True. It hadn't been painted yet and was still that run-down, pea-soup color chipped paint.

I thought back to my house and yard in its full Halloween glory. I smiled. It *was* pretty awesome. I made a split-second decision. "Sure."

His eyes widened. Apparently, that was not what he expected. "Really?"

I shrugged. "Why not?"

He leaned in. "I just really want to have an octopus tentacle coming out of my window."

"It is pretty cool," I said and smiled.

"And I also want to do this," he said softly before he kissed me.

Another fringe benefit of helping him.

When we broke apart, he stuck his hand out to shake. "So, we have a deal?" he asked.

I shook his hand. "Deal," I said. "But you're not planning on starting right now, are you?"

"No," he said.

"Want to stay and watch a movie? I have microwave popcorn."

He didn't let go of my hand. Instead, he settled into the couch beside me. "I hoped you'd say something like that."

OCTOBER

22

KATE

Grant and I sat in the two Adirondack chairs in his front yard, sipping apple cider. A wooden spool served as our table. Midnight sat guard at the base of the table. Since the conversation about decorating his yard, we'd worked tirelessly.

I called it "Rise of the Skeletons". We had secured fake tombstones all around the front yard. Rising from the ground were skeletons, and glow-in-the-dark rats running from them. Bats and spiders and cobwebs hung between the trees, backlit with strings of black and orange and purple lights. Motion sensor howler devices were scattered about, a feature we'd probably both regret if the raccoons decided to explore the scene in the middle of the night. And last, but not least, we perched a huge cauldron in the middle of the wonderful scene filled with lights to shine on the motorized smoke machine and octopus tentacles coming out and the largest reaching out from the garage.

The transformation was nothing short of magnificent. His yard had gone from overgrown to spooktacular.

I had posted a couple of pictures of the progress on

Instagram. Even though I'd lost all my sponsors, I found I still liked to document my projects.

He held out his red Solo cup to mine and we tapped rims. "I'm scared to walk in my own yard. And that's a compliment."

"Thanks. You're not so bad yourself," I said. "If you want, we can bust out the jack-o-lanterns. Or the big, hairy blow-up tarantula spider."

He chuckled. "I think this will do."

"Are you sure? There's more we can do," I said.

"You do good work I'm not just talking about the yard. The house renovation stuff has been great."

His house had progressed in measurable ways since he'd moved in. The drywall had been replaced; the bathrooms remodeled. Once the flooring was installed, Grant moved his furniture out of his garage and into his house.

And best of all, I got to keep my furniture.

"I think the best thing of all is your brand-new central A/C," I said.

Grant nodded and took a sip. "I definitely appreciate that, but unfortunately, it's fall now and I won't need it as much. I hope my heater works, or I'll be back to visiting you every day."

I stared at him, stunned. "You didn't buy a heater unit as well?"

He laughed. "Of course, I did, but I couldn't miss an opportunity to tease you."

"Watch out. That teasing could come back and bite you in the butt," I said. Although, at the moment, I didn't have any plans to carry that threat out.

With cup in hand, he pointed to the garage. The big octopus tentacle spilled out at the corner of the building.

"Once I'm done with the house, I'm going to knock down the garage."

I drained the last of my lemonade through the straw with a loud slurp. "Really? It's not worth saving?"

"Originally, I thought I could. But the bats are so bad in there. There is so much poop in the attic it has caused sagging in the ceiling. It's a health hazard and I want to bulldoze it."

"Don't tell Chrissy, she'll ask to drive the bulldozer," I said.

"Maybe I'll let her. It's a tear-down, she can't do too much damage."

His phone rang and he fished it out of his pocket. He glanced the screen, pursed his lips and answered. "Hello?"

I watched his facial expressions.

"Speaking," he said.

He listened and slowly his eyebrows came together. Was it a scam call? An extended warranty on his car was about to expire? Bad news?

"I'm not sure. Let me think about it."

There was a pause, then he gave the caller his email address. "Thank you," he said and ended the call. He ran his hands through his hair and looked at me. "That was weird."

"What?"

"I was just offered a sick amount of money to rent my place out on Halloween for a party. They said they saw pictures of it on Instagram."

"Really? That's awesome!" I asked. It was definitely odd, but it still made me smile, because someone obviously liked my work. I hadn't even thought about the pictures I'd posted.

I pulled up my account and my mouth dropped open when I saw the comments. I had over five thousand likes.

And there were comments! I scrolled through the comments, still in shock that anyone had even seen my post.

Jwanna634: She's back????

Halloweenyteeny: Love it! Stealing it.

Halloweveobsessd: OBSESSED!

Michmamagirl: Décor inspo!

I still had fans?! "I still have fans!" I screamed.

I jumped up and did a happy dance, realized I looked ridiculous and sat back down immediately.

Grant startled from my sudden outburst. I was just as surprised with myself. I didn't think I cared that much that people still followed me. At least, I had tried to convince myself of that for the last few years. It hadn't worked.

He leaned over to get a closer look at my screen. "What?"

My heart beat so fast I put my hand on my chest to keep it from bursting out. "People still follow me. I'm shocked. It's been so long."

"That's good, right?"

My head bobbed. "Yes, it's really good." I honestly thought no one still cared.

StaceyStacieStacy: Let's do a collab!

"So that's where that person saw my house and yard."

I grabbed his arm. "Oh, my gosh, are you going to do it? It might be kind of cool." I was shocked that one person even still followed me, let alone five thousand. My imagination took over as I pictured a Halloween party, at night, with lights on, candles lit, dry ice smoking, eerie music playing. Almost made me want to host my own party. Almost.

"They offered me a crazy amount of money," Grant said.

I clapped my hands in quick succession. "You should totally do it," I said.

I still had it.

People still liked my stuff.

People still liked me.

"Grant, that is so cool!"

"And he said something about media releases."

"Okay, and?" I asked.

Maybe it was just because I was *slightly* desperate for money and on a high from how great Grant's house turned out, but I would totally take it as a compliment if I'd gotten the same call Grant had. I saw no downside to it at all.

23

GRANT

The man named Kelly with platinum blonde hair stood in my living room, with his index pressed to his lip, staring at my ceiling. I stood beside him, trying to figure out what exactly he was looking at. The water stains?

He turned. "This is perfect. Perfect."

After our phone call, he'd come out to my house to check the "suitability" of the "site". I didn't know what to expect, but it certainly wasn't this. He came armed with a dinged-up, foam board, pictures attached to it and clear packing tape down the middle, holding two halves together.

"Obviously, we love the outside. Inside we envision a haunted house for the guests to walk through," Kelly said. "Originally, we were having the wedding at the amusement park in town, but power went out, computers glitched, reservations were lost and boom!" He made an explosion motion with his hands. "My otherwise very...*sweet*...client went into bridezilla mode and it was literally very scary for a couple of days. Thank goodness I saw your house on Instagram. It took a little bit of research to find your number, but I'm so glad I did. You've saved the wedding."

"I don't know if the house will be finished in three weeks. I still have interior and exterior painting, cabinets, the outside steps, the driveway and a punch list of other things I can't even remember." Even with the newly added help from Kate, there was still a lot of work to be done.

"The unfinished look isn't a problem and will work for what we have planned. And we'll hire a team to finish anything necessary for the wedding. If you're okay with that."

Someone else doing the work for me? Sure, I was fine with that!

"They'll exit out the back door and have the ceremony outside." He sashayed to the back door and swung it open. "Mind if I have a look?"

I followed him. "Just be careful of the first step. It's rotten and I don't want you to fall through."

We went down the steps and stopped in the yard. Kelly clucked, inhaled and resumed walking. "Maybe the side yard has more space," he said.

When Mira and I got married, it was all very traditional. In a church, reception followed in a banquet hall. Honestly, I had no idea themed weddings were a thing. I knew Kate had planned a Halloween wedding. I'd have to check out her YouTube channel and see if there were any videos with it. I was curious.

"Now, that's a beauty."

I stopped where he stopped: the back of my garage. Admittedly, I didn't see anything beautiful. The windows were still broken, the roofline sagging. I couldn't wait for my house to be done so demo could start on this.

"It's an eyesore."

"It's perfect. That's where we could do the ceremony," Kelly said.

"There're bats," I said.

Kelly didn't blink. "We'll hire someone to take care of the bats."

"I don't think it's structurally sound. In fact, I was going to demo it once renos with the house were finished."

He snapped his fingers and walked forward, rounded the corner and walked to the front. "I'm having an idea. If you're going to knock this down, could we modify it and use it?"

Too bad he didn't want to knock it down and build me a new one. "Modify it how?"

"First we'll open it up a bit, paint it black." He moved along the side until he came to the garage door. "And keep the tentacle, because I love that." He snapped a few pictures from different angles. "Remove the door, have the trellis here. I love it."

"And you're going to pay *me* to do that?" That was free labor in my book.

"Yes. If you agree. I'll have the details spelled out in the contract. As soon as you sign, we'll get a construction crew in here. They'll finish what needs to be finished, build what needs to be built, and modify what needs to be modified. It'll be stunning."

I couldn't catch his vision. But the dollar signs on the contract caught my attention.

When the contract was emailed to me later that day, I didn't think twice about signing on the dotted line.

∼

THREE DAYS LATER, PICK UP TRUCKS AND CARS LINED MY driveway. Men in fluorescent green t-shirts emerged, ready to work. Equipment was unloaded, wood was delivered and projects started. I wish I had signed up for this sooner, it would've saved me a lot of work.

New steps were built in the back, leading into a wooden archway/path/trellis/whatever that led to the back wall of the garage. Holes were cut, landscape leveled, trash removed. It was the synchronization of a well-oiled machine and all I had to do was sit back and watch it happen.

Having nothing better to do with myself, I went to Kate's.

We got comfortable next to each other on the couch. "You must've said yes to the party. Either that or you or Bill won the lottery and can pay someone else to finish the work."

"I'm letting them rent out the place. They'll do the construction work they need finished for the wedding and I get to keep the finished project."

"Wait. It's a wedding?" she asked.

"Yeah. A Halloween wedding. I never knew it was such a thing until I met you."

"It seems to be a popular night for weddings in town. My ex is supposed to get married at the Gainesville Amusement Park that night."

An uneasy feeling settled over me. "Really? How'd you know that?"

"Chrissy works at the park."

Kelly's words rang through my head. *Originally, we were doing the wedding at the amusement park in town, but power went out, computers glitched, reservations were lost and boom! The client went into bridezilla mode.*

I untangled myself from her. "I just realized I need to do something."

"Oh," she said, then sniffed her armpits. "Do I smell bad or something and you don't want to tell me the truth?"

"Nope," I said and kissed her forehead. "You smell delicious. I'll be back over later."

I hurried home and up the stairs to my room. Upstairs was the only place inside that was off-limit to the strangers in the house.

What was the name of Kate's fiancé? I knew his first name was Sean, but didn't have a last name. I pulled up Kate Renovates on YouTube.

There were links to her website and most of her social media accounts. I clicked on Instagram and scrolled through until I found one with her, a guy and a shiny diamond ring. I clicked on the tagged account of the guy she was kissing.

Sean Amatino

Whose wedding was at my house again?

I pulled up the contract, skimming until I found the names.

Merry Webber.

And Sean Amatino.

Oh, crap.

24

GRANT

I'd have to face Kate sooner or later. Later sounded better, but sooner would get it out of the way.

I didn't want to tell her.

Maybe I wouldn't have to tell her.

But what if she saw someone she recognized?

Was it better to make a preemptive strike and tell her the truth?

It wasn't like I was purposely being dishonest.

I wanted to spare her the pain.

I wanted to protect her.

But she'd probably find out and then she'd be mad at me.

Life was complicated, but women were even more complicated.

I didn't want the relationship between Kate and I to be complicated.

I wrestled with what to do.

I returned to her house a while later, still weighing the pros and cons that had kept me at my house.

"I have a dilemma," I said, my voice quiet.

She held my hand and stroked the top of my thumb with hers. "What's going on?"

"You know that wedding party that rented out my place? I think I should cancel with them, but I'm not sure I can."

"What? Why? You need the money...so you can pay me. *I* need the money."

I cleared my throat. "It's more complicated than just the money."

"How can it be more complicated than that? You let them rent your place for twenty-four hours and they pay you. I wished someone had called me about doing it at my house, even though yours is obviously way more apropos for the job. I would've said yes in a heartbeat.

No, she wouldn't have. "It's Sean's wedding."

The rubbing stopped. Her eyes widened and her mouth fell open. "That can't be. They're getting married at the amusement park."

"The wedding planner guy—"

"Kelly," she said.

"Yes, Kelly—wait. How did you know?" And what else did she know?

"That was the reason I quit Hawley's Hobbies. I was supposed to work with Kelly on Merry's wedding. I refused."

Out of loyalty, would she expect me to refuse to work with them? Except for the problem of the already-signed contract.

I sighed. "He didn't tell me who his clients were, just that there was a mix-up at the park, his client saw the picture of my house and insisted they have it here."

"You can cancel, you know."

I wished. "Cancel how? I have a contract with them."

"I don't know. Make up an excuse. Tell them your cesspool is overflowing. That your basement flooded. That there's an angry mob of rabid raccoons running loose and you're worried for the safety and well-being of the guests."

I mentally reviewed the contract. I didn't remember any mention of overflowing cesspools or rabid raccoons. But I hadn't exactly read it closely and I didn't know if there were any loopholes to get out of it.

I didn't want to cancel on them. Not really. If it hadn't been Kate's ex, I wouldn't have given it a second thought. But I went into the situation not knowing, and now that I knew, I probably wouldn't be able to get out of it.

"Can you see the dilemma?" I asked, hoping for the best-case scenario and she'd understand.

She was silent.

"What are you going to do?" she asked.

I had mixed feelings about the situation. Obviously, I needed the money since this Haunty needed so much more work than originally expected.

"I don't know," I said.

Kate pressed her lips together and nodded.

I couldn't blatantly hurt Kate like that. Having her ex get married right next door to where she lives? Is that what the bride was intentionally doing? Kelly had explained that a power outage in town had caused a computer glitch and had canceled their reservation. Wouldn't a wedding be a big enough deal that the venue wouldn't "forget" about it?

Or maybe the bride wanted it someplace where Kate wouldn't miss it.

Who knew?

I looked at her, but she was staring off to the left. "What do you think?" I asked.

She shrugged and stood. "I don't know." Her voice had a bit of a hard edge to it. "It's your house. Do what you want."

"But I want your opinion," I said.

She picked up her cup, swirled it around and then dumped it out. "My opinion doesn't matter. Really."

The tone of her voice changed, clueing me in that this could easily turn into a fight. I had slowly broken down some of Kate's walls since I moved here and I was worried that in no time, she'd throw them back up again. I didn't want to lose the traction we'd made.

I liked the new Kate. She was happier, more dynamic than when I'd met her. She wasn't back to the Kate on her YouTube channel (yes, I'd watched a couple more), but I didn't want her to be. She'd grown into a different version of Kate. One that I was falling for.

Hard.

I didn't want to betray Kate, but I really needed that money. My house—Mira's dream—needed that money.

I stood too, and reached for her elbow. "I'm trying to do the right thing, Kate."

She shook it off. "I'll talk to you later," she said and walked off.

Somehow, without meaning to, I became the bad guy.

25

KATE

Well, that sucked.

Basically, he betrayed me.

But, in his defense, he didn't know who he was renting it to.

Technically, not his fault.

But I'd be lying if I said it didn't bother me.

A LOT!

Part of me wanted to go over to his cesspool and overflow it myself. Then Sean and Merry's wedding would literally stink. What would it take? Leave a hose running next to it so it flooded the area? Flush a box of tampons down his toilet, one at a time, until the plumbing literally wasn't working? I didn't want it to cost Grant, I wanted it to cost *them*.

I plopped down on my couch and looked around for Midnight. Petting her and brainstorming ways to ruin their day would definitely calm me down. Okay, not ruin it. Just add a hiccup to their plans, a wrinkle to their wedding.

After a few days, I was still agitated. I'd managed to

avoid Grant, but that didn't make me feel better. I felt like a caged panther, pacing, my freedom out of my control. I didn't like it. Instead of stewing, I needed to take action. And the best way to feel back in control was ~~revenge~~ find a project to work on. Finding a job was also on that list, but it was too easy to feel defeated. I needed to avoid anything negative in my life.

Determined to distract myself, I went on the hunt for a piece of furniture to paint. Surely, I had something tucked away somewhere…

In the corner of my She Shed, on top of the unstocked mini fridge, there was a small wooden magazine holder circa 1970's holding some folded-up drop cloths. That would do. The only fresh paint I had was Kiss and Teal, so my choice was made for me. I set up my work area, and my camera to film it, and started painting. An hour later I had a finished piece and felt less frustrated. I needed more pieces. What else did I have around? My eyes spied a wooden ladder, folded up, leaning against the wall. Ah ha! My next project.

As much as I loved Kiss and Teal, it wasn't the perfect color for every project. I needed some white paint. And some black paint. I needed to go to Home Depot.

I'd eventually run out of things to paint from my personal stash.

Was there any free furniture on the online marketplace?

That had been one of my go-to sources way back when. Usually there was one or two (or more) pieces of furniture people wanted gone. I fired up my laptop and started the search.

Luck was on my side. There was a small dresser and matching night stand. I messaged the seller and then set off to Home Depot. I felt almost…elated.

If the Broom Fits

173

~

WHEN I RETURNED HOME, I FELT BETTER. I HAD PAINT, I HAD pieces...I had a dresser jammed in the backseat of my car that I would need help getting out.

I convinced myself I could get it out myself, but proved myself wrong.

I glanced over at Grant's yard, work crews busy prepping for the big day. The steady rhythm of progress punctuated the air: nail guns, saw blades, paint sprayers. Grant was nowhere in sight. He would be my logical go-to person, but I wasn't ready to see him yet.

I wonder if I could grab one of those guys to help me.

With help, it could be out in under five minutes. I was sure of it.

Looking around once more to make sure Grant wasn't around and walked up to the first guy I came to in a fluorescent green shirt. Waterberry Construction was printed in black letters on the back.

"Excuse me, would you be able to help me lift something for a minute?" I asked.

When he turned around, I recognized him immediately.

He also recognized me. "Oh, look, it's the witch."

"What are you doing here?" It was very unexpected and caught me off guard.

"I work here. What are you doing here?"

I assumed he graduated high school way back when, but obviously wasn't super smart. "I live here. You're not going to ruin the wedding, are you? Graffiti the altar or something?"

"I work a legit job, as you can tell," he said, but then smiled an evil smile. "You always assume the worst of me."

"Your track record says otherwise," I said.

"People change."

Of course, I didn't believe him. "Do they?"

Was I the same person I was when he'd first attacked ol' Haunty? No. Was he? Who knew? But I didn't care enough to find out. I still didn't trust him. And I didn't trust him to invite him onto my property to help me. Who knew what sort of vandalism I'd be opening myself up for?

But...maybe I needed to give the kid a break. Maybe he had reformed since "The Incident". I decided to give him the benefit of the doubt, but not ask his help.

I walked past him without another word, looking for someone else who could help.

Grant's front door opened and he ran down the stairs. "Hey, Kate. Can we talk?"

There was no way out of this. I had to face him at some point, although I hoped that would be once I had gotten over the situation. But, no time like the presence to pull on my big girl panties and be an adult.

"Okay," I said, but my words were drowned out by a hammer.

"Okay!" I yelled louder.

"Can we go to your house where there's less noise?" he asked.

We walked to my house without saying a word. Once inside, Grant took a seat. "Listen, Kate, I'm sorry about the whole wedding thing. I made an honest mistake. Is there something I can do to fix this?"

I choked up a little. The emotions I'd held inside bubbled up and leaked.

He came over to me and wrapped his arms around me. "Kate," he said. "Don't cry."

I swiped at the tears. "I'm trying really hard not to." I hated crying. I cried so much after my wedding, I avoided crying. And yet here I was, blubbering into Grant's shoulder, boogers leaving their mark on his t-shirt. I hated weakness.

"Oh, sweet Kate," he said, his voice soothing.

"I'm not sweet," I said, my words muffled by his shoulder. "I'm not sweet. I'm a miserable person and..."

He put both hands on my shoulders and leaned down so he was at eye-level. "Kate, despite your faults, or anything else you think is wrong, I have still fallen for you."

I pulled away from him and sniffed. "Have the paint fumes gone to your head?"

He laughed. "Why? Because I have feelings for you?"

"Well, yeah. Pretty much."

"Isn't it time to banish the ghosts from the past and move on?"

I thought about it. Since Grant had moved in, I had moved on. And it hadn't been such a terrible, scary thing. Trusting myself again—and trusting him—was a slow process, but one that had been started.

"Give yourself a little leeway. Give me a little leeway. Let's figure out a way through this."

His kindness made me blubber again. I tried to sniff away the emotions that kept leaking out. I swiped my eyes. "Okay," I said.

He held me a little longer and I relaxed into him.

"I tried to look for ways to get out of this. I can't find a way," he said.

"I don't want to be around for it," I said.

"Maybe we don't have to be around for it. We could go out that day. Take a drive, make it a date."

After a few minutes, I had an idea. "Maybe we could take a day trip. There's a little town down the coast that I used to go antiquing at. If you'd be interested, we could go together."

Realizing I could leave and not watch the whole wedding unfold through binoculars at my window made me feel better. I could give Grant the benefit of the doubt that it was an honest mistake. I didn't think he'd intentionally hurt me.

"Count me in."

26

KATE

Grant's yard had transformed into a nightmare.

"I tell you, that girl doesn't have an original bone in her body," I said. "It's like déjà vu all over again from my wedding."

It was actually the day of the wedding, but it was fun to refer to it as a nightmare.

The leaves on the trees had turned and left a cover of red, orange, gold and amber on the ground. The color addition added a nice touch to the "Rise of the Skeletons", because now, instead of just rising from the ground, it created a kind of bloodbath effect. Obviously, the perfect look for any wedding.

It had cooled down to sweater weather and Grant and I frequently hung out on the porch to enjoy the fresh air. And each other. I had found a child-sized camping chair that suited Midnight's lounging needs perfectly. But since it was Halloween, she slept inside while we watched the wedding set-up frenzy from a safe distance on my front porch.

Grant took a drink from his coffee cup. "So this is really *The Nightmare Before Matrimony*."

I warmed my hands on my mug. "Or *Nightmare on Our Street*. Question is, whose nightmare?"

He leaned toward me. "The better question is: who cares?"

I leaned in also. "I know I don't."

And I didn't.

We closed in for a kiss, but was interrupted.

BA-BAM! BA-BAM! BA-BAM! Echoed loudly between the two houses.

"What're they doing?" I asked, turning away from the kiss.

"I don't know. Yesterday they spray-painted any exposed wood in the garage black. Kelly said they'd be hanging up the black spiderweb netting today."

They'd taken the garage back to the studs, except for the roof. "With everything they've removed, I wonder if it's structurally unsound," I said.

"That's what I thought. I pointed that out, even warned him that there was some dry rot, but Kelly said that's what Merry wants." Grant laughed a little. "He even pantomimed the scene of her stomping her foot. I don't think he's a fan of the bride."

"I understand," I said, then stood. "Should we pack the car?" I asked. Grant and I had a wonderful, leisurely day planned, which included lunch, shopping, and picking up a scratched-up vintage music cabinet and a small pie safe, courtesy of the online marketplace.

"Yeah. I'll go grab my jacket and some work gloves," Grant said. He gave me a quick kiss on the lips and headed home. I watched him as he walked, admiring him. It left a warm feeling in my chest.

I went to the She Shed and gathered some moving blankets, a tarp and some tie down straps. I wasn't sure how the two pieces would fit in the back of Grant's vehicle and wanted to be prepared just in case we needed to put one on the roof. I found my work gloves, threw everything in a canvas tool bag and locked up the She Shed.

Grant's Subaru was now parked in my driveway, and he stood by the ajar rear door. I set the bag in the back. "Should we bring more blanket?" I asked. "I don't want to scratch up your car."

He bobbed his head side-to-side, as if weighing the options. "Nah. I think it's okay."

"Great. Should we—"

A bright red Mustang accelerated up the still-dirt driveway toward Grant's house.

"What the heck?" Grant said.

When it was almost to the garage, it took a hard right, but didn't stop. Instead, it skidded on a blanket of wet leaves.

CRUNCH!

The car sideswiped the corner of the garage.

Grant craned his neck for a better look. "Did they just hit my garage?"

I stepped to the side to get a better look. "Sounds like something happened," I said.

He grabbed my hand. "Let's go check it out!"

Before I could answer, the driver's side door flew open and Merry Webber jumped out of the car. Her outfit surprised me. She wore lemon pajama pants, a black, silk robe with a bedazzled *BRIDE* on the back and her feet stuffed into a pair of UGG boots.

We stood stunned, wondering what was going on.

"She must be here to boss everyone around," I said and clucked my tongue. "Wonder where the film crew is."

Merry left the car door open and stomped off, not even stopping to look at the damage done to the car or the garage.

We hurried over to check out the garage.

Sure enough, Merry had hit the corner with her bumper, causing it to crumple a bit. It looked like she might've even taken a chunk out of the wood of the building.

Grant and I leaned down to take a closer look, but the activity just around the corner grabbed our attention.

"Just wait. Take a breath," Kelly said as he rushed up to Merry, his hands up, either trying to calm her down or stop her. She sidestepped him and marched on.

"Uh-oh," I said. "Someone's in trou-ble."

"What do you think they did?" Grant asked.

"Opened the box of spider webs and found out they accidentally ordered slime green instead of coffin black?" I suggested.

"Or, the person in charge of stringing up the lights dropped the whole box and all the lights shattered," Grant said.

I shrugged. "Or maybe *Bridezilla* is really coming to film and she wants to announce the news to everyone." I paused and thought about it. "But that doesn't make sense because wouldn't there be a camera shadowing her now?" I looked to see if I could get a better view of what was going on. "Really, it could be anything. She's a drama queen and drama follows her wherever she goes."

"ARE YOU KIDDING ME?" Merry's voice pierced the air.

Grant craned his neck to get a better look. "Whoa, what's going on?"

"Uh-oh," I said. "That sounds like serious trouble in paradise."

Behind us, another car sped up the driveway and skidded to a stop. And then another. Four women escaped out of the first car like cockroaches, passed us, then went behind the side of the house and out of sight. A variety of people, (presumably family because of the bright red hair) followed in the footsteps of the women.

With all the people hurrying by, there had to be an emergency.

"I've got to see this," I said.

I'll admit to being intrigued. Remembering all the drama Merry caused for my wedding, it'd be good for her to experience a little of the same.

"DON'T TELL ME IT'LL BE OKAY! THIS IS NOT OKAY!"

We hightailed it to the She Shed. Now we had the perfect view of the Grant's backyard. And the drama.

"THIS IS SO NOT OKAY!"

The area to the northwest side of the now bare-bones garage had tables lined up for the reception immediately after the ceremony. Catering crews were setting up tents to the north of the tables. Work men with hammers and staple guns and ladders were scattered about the lawn taking care of last-minute preparations.

The people who had just arrived now stood in a small semi-circle a few feet from the main event. Merry stood, in front of Sean and a blonde woman, shaking her fists in the air.

"SHE'S MY BEST FRIEND!"

The hum of work disappeared as silence settled over the workers standing witness.

Kelly appeared at my side without me noticing. "Ho-ly *crap*. Can you believe this?" he said, his hand dramatically on his forehead.

"Kelly! You scared me," I said.

"I KNEW IT! YOU WILL NEVER BE ABLE TO KEEP IT IN YOUR PANTS, WILL YOU?"

"What a disaster," he said, then looking away from the scene and around my She Shed. "Great space! You mind if I hide here?"

"Sure," I said. "The more the merrier."

He grinned tensely. "Thanks. Any chance there's a Cosmopolitan in that mini fridge?"

I laughed despite his palpable stress.

"No," I said. "What—"

CRRRR—

An odd noise punctured the air. A groan? A moan? Was it from someone in the circle?

Sean's hands waved as he talked. "Listen, Merry—"

It was a slow, splintering sound.

CREEEEAK!

As if in slow motion, the visible back corner of Grant's garage collapsed and the roofline began to cave.

"My garage!" Grant cried.

The three of us raced to the scene of destruction.

Moments later, another sound rang out.

BOOM! SMASH!

CRUNCH!

We stopped in our tracks and watched in fascinated horror as a massive section of the front corner of the garage buckled, and landed—

—on the Mustang's front end.

The sound of broken glass shattered the air.

Then *WHAP! WHAP! WHAP!* filled the air as a black, fluttering cloud scattered from the top of Grant's garage.

"AAAGH! BATS! BATS!"

The group of people fled in all directions.

When the dust settled, we were able to assess the actual condition of his garage.

Or what used to be his garage.

With a noise that could only be described as grating friction, the remaining slab of the roof slid down and landed with a thud on the ground, dumping something that looked like a layer of black pebbles from beneath it.

Broken pieces of wood stuck up at weird angles from the wreckage. And, as if signaling it had survived, the tentacle poked out from underneath the carnage.

"Oh, no," Grant said under his breath.

Kelly squirmed beside me, while Merry and Sean and the wedding party stood frozen off in the distance.

Kelly laid his hand on my shoulder. "Are you hiring?" he asked.

"It's not that bad," I lied, trying to soothe Kelly's distress.

Off in the distance, Merry continued raging. "DON'T YOU TELL ME—"

Kelly looked at his watch. "Sweetie," he said. "I'm calling the time of death as of...now."

"Merry! Please! Just listen—" Sean reached out to Merry.

"NO MORE!" Merry chopped Sean's hand from her elbow.

Family members gathered closer, presumably trying to intervene, but the ex-bride and groom were still going strong.

My mouth hung open. "What started it?" I asked.

"Merry caught Sean with her Maid of Honor, and... timber." Kelly whistled as he made a tipping gesture.

Grant looked pale. "Just like my garage."

"We'll clean it up, of course," Kelly said quickly.

"Uh, yeah. I sure hope so," Grant said.

"I'm pretty sure the wedding is over, and as soon as that's

confirmed, I'm going to have that Cosmo. Or three," Kelly said.

I pitied Kelly for a moment, but appreciated not being in his shoes.

I turned back to the fight in time to see Merry stalk off, leaving Sean and the Maid of Honor and the rest of the party standing awkwardly in the yard.

"Merry! Merry!" Sean called after her, having shaken off the shock of the moment.

"Guano, guano," one of the Hispanic workers called out, pointing as Merry approached the splintered pile formerly the roof. He held his hand out and tried to stop her as she walked by.

Merry clenched her fists and jerked her arms. "Oh, shut up and get out of my way!"

"Guano!" the worker warned one more time, in vain.

Merry marched past him, stepped in the pile of black "pebbles" and her right leg shot forward and her left foot slid, her body flailed as she lost balance, caught air and landed on her backside.

She lifted her stained hands from the ground, looked at them and screeched. "What is this?"

Sean raced over to offer his hand, but she brushed it aside, rolled over onto her hands and knees and stood up. Merry's girlfriends stood to the side of the pile, arms reached out to help her.

"Guano, ma'am," the worker said. "How do you say," his hand circled in the air, "bats poop."

Merry's face went from beet red to ashen. "I slipped in bat poop? That's disgusting!" she shook her hands frantically. "I could catch a disease!" With three steps sideways, she was out of the pile and back at her walk of shame, mumbling to herself, trailed by her friends.

Sean tried once again to slow her down. "Just let me explain," he said.

She slapped away his hand "Don't touch me!" she screamed, then grabbed at her ring finger. "Here, you swine," she held up the engagement ring and then turned and threw it in the guano. "Go dig in the bat poop."

He looked at her, then the Maid of Honor and then to the pile of guano, as if deciding what to do.

My mouth gaped open. Sean had cheated *again*. And the pile of bat poop just made it that much better.

I giggled, which turned into a whoop of laughter. Totally inappropriate, I knew, but couldn't help myself.

Suddenly, Merry froze.

Even from where I was, I could see her eyes grow wide as she stared at the roof, now on the ground.

She slowly scanned the area until our eyes met.

My heart stuttered in panic.

Merry's arm lifted until she pointed at me. "How dare you!" she screeched.

A small rumble of voices, chuckling, and some gasps could be heard. Wedding party members pointed at the crumpled, garage roof.

What were they looking at? Grant and I took a few steps forward before we saw it.

THE BRIDES A WITCH

The words were spray-painted in fluorescent orange letters across the shingles.

"Huh," I said smiled. That only could've been done by one person. Dirk the Delinquent. He must've thought from our brief conversation that *I* was the bride.

It was oddly satisfying that the guy who painted that thought he was somehow getting back at me, but instead ruined more of Merry's wedding. I started laughing.

"HOW DARE YOU SHOW YOUR FACE HERE!"

Screaming, Merry broke into a run.

Right toward me.

I stepped back, afraid that Merry was going to trample me, but she stopped because Grant threw himself between us.

"She lives here," he said, shielding me.

Sidestepping Grant, she continued yelling at me. "You don't live HERE!" She pointed at his house.

"No, I live next door. With your level of stalking, you should know that."

Merry bared her teeth. "You're not welcome at my wedding."

"From what I've seen, there isn't going to be a wedding," I said.

"And I bet you just love that. You're just enjoying it, rubbing it in, aren't you?"

I held my hands up and took another step back, putting some space between us. Even with Grant standing there, she was too much in my personal space. "No—"

"Shut up! I hate you!"

I held my hands up innocently. "I didn't say anything."

Her face twisted into a sneer. "Oh, but I can just hear you thinking that I deserve this."

Oh, how she deserved it.

I smiled pleasantly at her. "What can I say, Merry? Karma's a witch."

JANUARY

EPILOGUE
KATE

*A*fter Merry Webber almost single-handedly demolished Grant's garage, he decided it was time to start fresh. And I agreed.

The result was what could only be described as a Victorian carriage house.

Okay, it was a really fancy garage. But it was amazing. It had a two-car garage on each side and a covered carport in the middle.

It was a collaboration between Grant and I.

Kelly clapped his hands. "Places everybody, places!"

Five women and one man, all DIY-ers, scurried to their assigned work tables.

I smiled as I stood at the back of the new carriage house, inhaling the heavenly scent of new construction. Lumber, paint, it was nothing short of intoxicating.

It was also the new headquarters of Kate's Paints.

Kelly left the world of wedding planning and the stress that came with the job, and joined me as marketing director. Today was a photo shoot for the catalog. A thrill ran through me.

This is really happening.

While Kelly organized things, I grabbed a couple of packages by the door and snuck out. I struggled to get a good grip on the bigger of the two as I carefully crossed the yard to Grant's house.

Ol' Haunty wasn't so haunted any more. After the non-wedding, the exterior had been painted a silver-blue with grey trim and a navy front door. This girl definitely approved (and may have had some influence in) the color choice. And together, we had put the finishing touches on the inside.

I rang the doorbell and waited, admiring the pleasant chimes heard inside.

"Meow."

Midnight stood at my feet. I smiled at her as I set the large box down. "Hey, Middy, you out here exploring?"

Grant appeared from the side yard and walked up the porch stairs. "More like guarding the house. She brought in a dead mouse this morning." He leaned in and kissed me.

"Aww, that's sweet. She brought you a housewarming gift," I said.

He put his finger to his lips. "Shh. Don't tell her, but I put her gift in the garbage."

I pulled a wrapped gift from behind my back. "Well, I hope you don't do that with my housewarming gift."

"You got me a housewarming gift? What is it?" he asked.

I handed it to him. "Open it and see," I said.

He unwrapped the package carefully, revealing a wooden plaque with a map of the area decoupaged on it. He teared up. He swiped at his eyes and cleared his throat. "You did my map."

"I didn't want you to forget what brought us together," I said.

He pulled me in for a kiss. "Thank you," he said. "But I thought Mod Podge brought us together."

"It was," I said. "But it's weird to hang a bottle of Mod Podge on the wall."

Grant laughed, then pointed to the other wrapped box by my feet. "Is that also a housewarming gift?"

I nodded and pushed it over to him with my foot. "It is."

With a little less care, he ripped the wrapping off the box. "A new shop vac! Kate, you shouldn't have," he said.

I pulled the box back toward me. "You're right. I shouldn't have. I actually bought that for me and am officially giving you my old one. You know, the one you borrowed and never returned."

"Ha ha. If I gave it back, you wouldn't have an excuse to come see me," Grant joked.

I playfully punched his arm.

He pulled me into a warm embrace and kissed the top of my head. "I love you, Kate."

I looked into his eyes. "I love you, too."

After allowing myself to take in the moment, I pulled away. "But we still have to go to work today."

"Okay, boss," he said.

Hand-in-hand, we walked back to our garage.

Turned out that Grant was a not just a high school teacher, but a visual arts teacher, specializing in video and film. He had been promoted from DIY house renovator to director of filming for Kate's Paints.

And he had also been promoted from annoying neighbor to boyfriend.

There was talk of further promotions, too.

Hopefully Kelly would agree to come out of retirement to help plan one more wedding.

Ours.

MORE BOOKS BY SALLY JOHNSON

The Suddenly Single Series

Suddenly Single (previously published as
The Skeleton in My Closet Wears A Wedding Dress)
Worth Waiting For
Anxiously Engaged (coming soon)

The Wit and Whimsy Romance Series

If the Kilt Fits
If the Boot Fits
If the Suit Fits
If the Broom Fits

Standalone Romances

Dear Mr. Darcy
Pretty Much Perfect
That Thing Formerly Known As My Life

ABOUT THE AUTHOR

Sally Johnson has written nine novels, the latest of which is *If the Broom Fits*. She enjoys watching classic rom-coms, but movies like *Notting Hill*, *About a Boy*, and *The Wedding Singer* have inspired her quest to explore real life relationships in humorous but grounded fiction.

When not writing, she taxis her kids around, dog-sits, and thrift-shops like a fiend.

For more books and updates, visit *SallyJohnsonWrites.com*

Sally would love to hear from you on social media!

- facebook.com/SallyJohnsonAuthor
- instagram.com/SallyJohnsonWrites
- amazon.com/author/johnson
- pinterest.com/sallysbj

Made in the USA
Coppell, TX
17 October 2021